"Every speech, news conference, presentation, media interview or quarterly conference call represents a potential risk and a potential opportunity. I can say without reservation that Anne Cooper Ready is simply the best coach when it comes to minimizing these risks and maximizing these opportunities."

—Kevin Brett
Director, Corporate Public Relations, LSI Logic
and former gubernatorial Press Secretary

"*Off the Cuf: What to Say at a Moment's Notice* is a practical guide for anyone who's anyone in the public eye—or anyone who wants to be. Anne Cooper Ready hits the mark."

—George David Kieffer, Esq.
Partner, Manatt, Phelps & Philips
Author, *The Strategy of Meetings*

"Anne Cooper Ready's to-the-point, down-to-earth tips on speaking extemporaneously are a Godsend to anyone who's ever felt lock jawed with panic at the thought of standing in front of a roomful of listeners. With humor, common sense, and years of professional insight, she helps turn a universally dreaded experience into an opportunity for even the most nervous speaker to shine."

—Stacy Ivers
Vice President, Strategic Communications
Warner Bros. Pictures

"Anne Cooper Ready helped me have fun with my toast and make it my own."

—Melanie Vance, Maid of Honor

"Anne Cooper Ready's new book *Off the Cuff: What to Say at a Moment's Notice* shoots down the myth that impromptu speaking means ad-libbing, speaking off the top of your head, or winging it without preparation. Smart speakers never wing it.

"This book should be on everyone's desk; everyone, that is, who doesn't want to sound stupid when asked to 'say a few words.' The insights give you an intelligent blueprint for organizing your ideas in the myriad of situations when you might be asked to speak 'off the cuff.'"

—Fred LaCosse
Veteran TV News Anchor

"One never knows when one needs to be in front of an audience and must say something intelligent. Anne Cooper Ready is the pro's COACH. Her easy-to-take advice combined with expertise perfected over the past 20-plus years has given me the confidence to respond in the spotlight."

—Patty DeDominic
Founder & CEO
PDQ Careers.com

"Met with the challenge of hiring talent who had little to no experience with on-camera interviews, I asked Anne Cooper Ready and Ready for Media to provide the tools and coaching to give our talent the confidence they needed. The process was quick yet thorough, in a comfortable, non-threatening environment."

—Ivey Van Allen
Vice President, Media Relations
Twentieth Television

Off the Cuff

What to Say at a Moment's Notice

By

Anne Cooper Ready

CAREER
PRESS
Franklin Lakes, NJ

OFF THE CUFF
EDITED AND TYPESET BY KRISTEN PARKES
Cover design by Cheryl Cohan Finbow

Graphical elements © 2003 www.clipart.com

To order this title, please call toll-free 1-800-CAREER-1 (NJ and Canada: 201-848-0310) to order using VISA or MasterCard, or for further information on books from Career Press.

The Career Press, Inc., 3 Tice Road, PO Box 687,
Franklin Lakes, NJ 07417
www.careerpress.com

Library of Congress Cataloging-in-Publication Data

Ready, Anne Cooper, 1948-
    Off the cuff : what to say at a moment's notice / by
Anne Cooper Ready.
        p. cm.
    Includes index.
    ISBN 1-56414-713-4 (paper)
    1. Extemporaneous speaking. 2. Public speaking. I. Title.

PN4168.R43 2004
808.5'1--dc22

2003065481

To my parents,

Mary Ann and Joe Cooper,

with great appreciation!

Acknowledgments

For their generous contribution of time and talent, I would especially like to thank Thomas Snyder, Olivia Burtis, Stephen D. Clouse, my agent Gene Brissie, Kristen Parkes, Kirsten Beucler, Anne Brooks, Stacey Farkas, Mike Lewis, Ron Fry, Randy Mell, Ed Coghlan, Grant Albrecht, Lansing Moran, Rebecca Street, Intel's Dr. Tracy Koon, Kim Scarborough, Gabe Mountain, W. Henry Walker, Bob Shober, Marge Bernstein, Sue Colin, Ph.D., and the Reverend Charles and Claire West Orr.

For their votes of confidence, I also wish to thank Regis Philbin, Spencer Johnson, M.D., Edward Roski, Jr., Allen N. Weiner, Kevin Brett, George David Kieffer, Stacy Ivers, Melanie Vance, Fred LaCosse, Patty DeDominic, and Ivey Van Allen.

And my great appreciation to all of the clients who have taught me while I have taught them.

Contents

Part II
Just Say a Few Words

Introduction

The phrase *off the cuff* is believed to have originated with waiters who were among the first to use their shirt cuffs as notepads to take orders or to calculate the tab. Hollywood directors were the next perpetrators of the practice, carrying notes to actors about the scene on their shirtsleeves.

Impromptu speaking has likewise become known as *off the cuff.* The speaker is pictured as hurriedly jotting down notes on his cardboard-starched shirt cuff during the meal and delivering them afterwards from an arm's-length note card.

When you think about it, almost every word we ever speak is spoken off the cuff, at a moment's notice, without anything but an intention. So, why a book on the subject?

The art of putting words together to communicate is something we are asked and expected to do on many occasions, from formal after-dinner speeches, wedding toasts, product presentations, and eulogies to informal opportunities such as news coverage with a media sound bite, a job interview, or an introduction of two friends. Knowing what to say and how to say it defines who we are, makes and breaks both friendships and careers, navigates you through office politics, and distinguishes you among your colleagues and competition. Speaking off the cuff can be learned and, with practice, perfected. It is just another arrow in your quiver of life skills.

PART I

Business Is a Contact Sport

The Number-One Fear

To conquer fear is the beginning of wisdom.
—Bertrand Russell,
philosopher and mathematician

Public speaking is listed as American's number-one fear, before death at number five, and loneliness, weighing in at number seven. Guess that means that most of us are less afraid of dying alone than of making fools of ourselves in front of others. Fear is a powerful motivator for leadership, which means that you stand above the crowd. There is the fear of being seen as exceptional and different; the fear of the unknown; the fear of being a fraud; the fear of forgetting everything you were going to say; the fear of being at risk publicly; and the fear of being up there, alone. They all come together, for most of us, in public speaking.

Some people believe that fear of standing up in public is about setting yourself up to be shot down. Much as John F. Kennedy and Robert Kennedy, Abraham Lincoln, Martin Luther King, Jr., and John Lennon were. Analogous to being a leader, standing up in

front of crowds to enlighten, incite, entertain, inspire, and lead
is what public speaking is all about. You are in good company.

The Chicken or the Egg

Motivational psychologists theorize that the fear of public
speaking comes from how the "show off" aspect of your personality was treated when you were a youngster. To what degree were you discouraged from performing in front of others?
Plus, bad experiences, such as freezing up in 4th grade when
reciting the Gettysburg Address, seems to compound the fear
and self-doubt.

But there's no going back to grade school to erase an
experience. A good solution to the regret and bad memories
comes from former *Los Angeles Times* publisher Jim Bellows,
"Begin at once and do the best you can."

Francis Bacon penned, "Nil terribile nisi ipse timor" ("Nothing is terrible except fear itself."). Henry David Thoreau
weighed in with, "Nothing is so much to be feared as fear."
Shakespeare wrote both that "extreme fear can neither fight
nor fly," and "cowards die many times before their deaths."
Mark Twain said, "Courage is resistance to fear, mastery of
fear—not absence of fear."

Note that these learned people were familiar enough with
fear to say something profound about it. So if misery loves
company, take comfort. Accomplished people are clearly not
strangers to fear. Obviously, they have met fear and if not mastered it, at least managed it enough to have achieved great things.

People who do speak up, and most of us do in one way or
another, seem to prefer courage to the cowardly alternative. A
Nobel laureate, physicist, and chemist, Madame Curie said,
"Nothing in life is to be feared, it is only to be understood." And
the solution reached by science fiction writer Doug Horton was
"Action cures fear, inaction creates terror." "The death of
fear is in doing what you fear to do," concluded the Cherokee

philosopher, Sequichie Comingdeer. While "No guts, no glory" became the battle cry of World War II.

Battle cries, quotations, advertising slogans ("Just do it"), headlines, song titles and good sound bites have an economy of words that say volumes to drive us in battle, propel us to buy, and give meaning in a world that doesn't walk its talk. When you are afraid, take this kind of less-is-more approach. First, make sure that your main points are cogent and concise. Second, create an outline and stick with it to keep yourself from rambling. Third, breathe. Focused, rhythmic, and slow breathing is usually helpful in calming those feelings of terror. Fourth, don't squelch the butterflies (or try to drown them in wine or sedatives, either).

Remember that fear is energy. Marshall your fear as energy to rise to the occasion. By organizing your thoughts logically and taking time to practice putting words to them, you will help get those butterflies flying in formation. And finally, enjoy the moment. This is one of the rare opportunities you have in life to speak to a captive audience, to tell people what you think and what you've learned to empower, motivate, inspire, soothe, or fascinate them.

Practice

Now, practice, practice, practice. There's an interesting paradox in public speaking. If you haven't practiced, you will appear nervous. But if you have practiced until it is second nature to say these words with expression, gestures, emphasis, and passion, you will appear spontaneous, as if you are speaking "off the cuff."

Dr. Sue Colin, a holistic therapist, once told me that one way to keep from getting sucked in by fear and mired in the muck of self-doubt is to keep your perspective as an observer. Keep noticing and noting what you observe. To allay your fears, keep a journal of the speakers you hear, which is almost everyone. How did someone answer the phone? Was she smiling when she recorded her voice-mail message? How could you tell? How did someone introduce himself? Did he make eye contact and seem happy to meet you? Did a conversation interest or bore you? Turn you off? Turn you on? Why? Did someone give a good TV interview? Become a critic—a constructive one. Offer a constructive critique, at least in your journal. What would you tell these communicators to do more, better, or differently? Be sure to tell yourself, too!

Television is a great source for impromptu conversation. Watch it constructively, to learn. A press conference or multi-city satellite tour is held to get the story to everyone at once. A speech happens for the same reason. The bigger the audience, the more people there are who want to hear you.

What do you admire and respect about the network news anchors who give a 30-minute speech every evening and throughout every national disaster? What is their take? Are they real? Do they get the irony or the impact? Do they like themselves? The viewing audience? The job? How do you know? Do you like them? Why or why not?

What can you take from the communications skills of these professionals? What can you learn from their ability to communicate? What can you do to improve your communication?

What about the late-night television comedians or the morning talk-show hosts? Who can you listen to year after year like Regis Philbin, Katie Couric, Johnny Carson, Leno, or Letterman? Why are they fun to watch?

Not that you're going to become a TV anchor or a comedian, but you are going to have to command a captive audience and you don't want them wishing they could change channels. In an age of channel surfing, you have to hold an audience's attention and interest.

So, you must know your audience. What do they want from you? What do they have a right to expect? What role do they play in this situation: conference attendees, a prospective employer, wedding guests, or a board of directors? What are their demographics in terms of age, region of the country, positions in the company, and expertise on your subject? The better you know them, the more you will have conquered the fear of the unknown. Television companies spend billions on audience research—common sense and deductive reasoning will go along way in helping you figure out your audience.

Passion and Purpose

If beliefs inspire behavior, behavior creates habits, habits influence character, and character dictates destiny, then beware your beliefs. You're only as good as your beliefs will let you be.

As a speechwriter and communications coach, I've always preferred clients who are afraid to those who are indifferent or just don't care. The energy of fear can be redirected to work *for* instead of *against* you. Indifference lacks the passion needed to get the message across. And it's all about putting the message, or the news, or the song, or the scene across.

An energy quotient I devised is that energy equals excitement plus enthusiasm. Ralph Waldo Emerson once said that nothing great was ever achieved without enthusiasm. Not that you necessarily have to be a cheerleader, but get in touch with your passion for the topic and for this particular audience. What makes your point of view exciting for you and for them? What makes it worth talking about? Let it be invigorating. Look deep into your fears, and that is where you will find your excitement. It is where you'll find the energy to be great!

As soon as you are asked to speak, even to say a few words, you are being acknowledged as someone who has something to say. You appear as someone to whom people should listen, someone who has been chosen to stand, in front of everyone, and deliver!

So, live it up. Have something important to say. And don't let your fear stop you. If not now, then when?

Self-Consciousness

The best antidote for fear is not to be self-conscious or conscious of self. Don't think about what you hope to *get* (a job, money, sales, popularity, admiration, or acclaim). Instead, be conscious of what you have to *give*. By concerning yourself with what you can contribute to your audience member's opinions, their knowledge, their valuable time, their lives, you give yourself a mission. Simply offer it in the best way you can.

Peggy Noonan, a contributor for *Good Housekeeping* and one-time speechwriter for President Ronald Reagan (who became known as the Great Communicator), explains that she conquered her own fear of public speaking by wanting to be understood. In short, she wanted to connect with her audience and get her anecdotes across.

Conquer your self-consciousness by getting outside of yourself and seeing how the audience is doing, one person at a time. A good speech should merely be one-on-one conversations with a hundred or a thousand people at a time. Don't scan the audience but make solid eye contact with six or so in different parts of the room.

Connect with those in the audience who make you feel most comfortable. Audiences usually fall into two categories, the "Smilers" and the "Stoics."

I prefer to talk with the Smilers, the ones who are responding and eager to learn, or at least listen to, what I have to say. They give me reassurance that what I am saying is important to them. One of my colleagues prefers the Stoics to the Smilers. "Smilers can be misleading," he will tell you. "They will smile and nod at everything. It's their social mode. Involve the Stoics, those who are looking at their shoes or the ceiling," he advises, "and you will really have accomplished something."

You can only please all of the people some of the time, and some of the people all of the time. But, of course, you can't please all of the people all of the time, ever.

Most of us learned from our parents that lectures don't work. Give your audience stories, examples, and quotes, organized around a main point with three supporting points that everyone can take home. One of the best sound bites I ever heard was, "The three most important things to remember are . . ."

Another good sound bite was delivered by two of my clients, Dr. Spencer Johnson and Ken Blanchard, authors of *The One Minute Manager*. They premiered their national media tour on Labor Day 1982 on *The Today Show* with the answer: "One Minute Management is three things, One-minute goal setting, one-minute praises and one-minute reprimands. One-minute goals are goals you can review in a minute." That was the beginning of a year-and-a-half run as the number one book on the *New York Times* Best-Seller List.

Self-Confidence

It may be a relief to know that even though you bring a certain expertise or perspective to the subject or occasion, it isn't really about you after all. As the speaker, you are only the messenger. But they shoot messengers, don't they? So how do you manage to keep your confidence?

Replace your fears with logical reasons to be confident and take every opportunity you can to speak and reinforce the fact that you speak well. There is a Hasidic saying, "The man who has confidence in himself, gains the confidence of others." What you put out there is going to reflect back to you.

So, create for yourself a sense of well-deserved confidence in your perspective, your expertise, your determination, your research, your experience, whatever you bring to the party. When I interviewed for my first job in television, I offered my experience with the TV show as a viewer and I got the job!

Sophia Loren said, "Getting ahead in a difficult profession requires avid faith in yourself. That is why some people with mediocre talent, but with great inner drive, go much further than people with vastly superior talent." Use your drive, your energy, your humor, and your thoughts to capture the crowd.

Plan carefully, practice well, and be confident that you have something to say and know how to say it. In other words, give yourself reason to be confident; then fake it, until you make it. Otherwise, your fear will first frighten an audience, then anger, then bore them. And nobody likes to be frightened, angry, or bored.

Fear is contagious. In days of old, the entire herd would "get it" in a fight-or-flight situation. When audiences perceive that you are very afraid, they are often ready to flee. The obvious next reaction is anger at your putting them in peril. And then boredom sets in because it's all about you and there's nothing in it for them. Every audience, in fact all of us, continually listen to WII-FM (What's In It For Me?).

You have both the absolute right and the perpetual responsibility not to bore an audience or waste its time. To paraphrase my mother's wisdom, "If you can't say something interesting, don't say anything at all!"

Your job, should you choose to accept it, is to make sure that you don't trip yourself up. Don't you hinder the message or cloud the communication and thus deserve being shot. Remember that this really isn't about you.

One Sunday after church, a pastor was praised on his sermon, with the suggestion that his eloquence must be the reason so many people attend his church. With humility and wisdom, he said that the reason both he and the congregation attend church is to praise God. "We just have different roles in the process."

Avoid taking yourself or the audience or the event too seriously. Turn your self-consciousness into self-confidence. Be prepared and then just use your butterflies for excitement and energy. Remember that you've been talking for years!

At a Moment's Notice  2

I dream about painting. Then just remember the dream and paint.

—Vincent Van Gogh

The secret to good ad-libbing is that it really isn't impromptu at all. It isn't usually just made up, offhand, on the spot, or at the last minute. It is thought about, organized, experimented with, researched, experienced, tried out, and practiced, practiced, practiced till the ideas are part of you, long before you stand to deliver.

Notice that I didn't say *written down*. The problem with writing anything down is that it often never comes *up* off of the page. It gets stuck there. Interesting ideas that are never communicated. Only very seasoned actors can make a cold read come alive. And notice, by the time the dress rehearsal comes along, the script has long since been put away and the art comes from the heart.

It's okay to note a list of words or phrases on a 3 x 5 card that will serve as talking points, but don't write down what you want to say and try to memorize it. Talk about it out loud, over and over, until you know it. Speaking is called speaking, not reading. Don't make the mistake of telling your thoughts to the page or scraps of paper and then reading them to your audience.

And even if you are still in the process of becoming a pro, you do have one advantage over people with professional speechwriters. Because you've come up with the words yourself, you know what is there. You cared about saying it. It's often been said that "no one cares how much you know until they know how much you care." Your words must come from the heart. Isn't that where our everyday speaking comes from anyway? From inside. You have an idea, a thought, an emotion that needs to be expressed. It has been said, don't seek to inform; seek to persuade, entertain, or motivate. Good speaking requires passion to make its point!

Be Ready...

...And don't be surprised. If there's any chance that you will or could be expected to "say a few words," have them ready beforehand. Years of readying clients for their 15 minutes of fame have shown me how important it is to be prepared, whenever called upon. Far better to leave with prepared remarks that weren't needed than to be asked to say a few words and not be primed to do it intelligently, with grace and good humor.

Also, when you are prepared in advance, you will find that opportunities to communicate, with self-confidence, will find you. Audiences are looking for speakers, followers for leaders.

Every public address needs a point of view. It's more than a topic, it's your opinion, your take, your advice; in short, the spin you put on your subject.

Like the perfect quote or sound bite, every word gives meaning to the whole and must have reason to be there. Do not go off on tangents. Not only do the words need a reason to be there, so does the speech. What is its reason for being? What job do you want it to do? What do you need to say to make that happen?

Be on Purpose

What do you want the people to know? What can you contribute to the moment?

Organize your material in a way that the audience can absorb it, not just hear it. A Zen Master often reminded his students that they would forget the lessons until they remembered the stories. Aesop did it with his famous fables. Who can forget the moral of slow and steady wins the race from *The Tortoise and the Hare*, of union gives strength from *The Bundle of Sticks*, or beware lest you lose the substance by grasping at the straws from *The Dog and the Shadow*?

Be Thankful...

Be thankful for a captive audience. The next time you are called upon to speak spontaneously, welcome the fact that you won't be interrupted by an interviewer, a therapist, and, hopefully, not even a cell phone.

The Cs of Communication

3

Keep It Simple, Sweetheart

The KISS principle of keeping it simple is more important than ever in today's fast-paced, sound bite–oriented world of communication. Make sure you don't tell your audience how to build a watch in answer to the question: What time is it?

The Cs of Communication

Conciseness is just one of the Cs of Communication, which also include: Conversational; Careful; Candid; Cogent; Convincing; Confident; Clear; Compassionate; Cool, Calm, and Collected; Correct; Compelling; Consistent; Credible; and Crisis

Conscious. Along with Controversial, which often gets you quoted. And, of course, Charismatic.

Concise

Blaise Pascal wrote: "I have made this letter longer than usual because I lack the time to make it short." By asking, "How much time do we have?" you put boundaries around the communication. How often is the game over when the pitcher has finally warmed up? Audiences appreciate respect for their time and will pay more attention when the end is in sight.

In a media interview, you should limit the time, too. Early in his career, Tiger Woods spent too much time with *Gentleman's Quarterly* and told more than he should have. So did a well-respected but controversial builder in Los Angeles who got himself in deeper and deeper in a six-hour interview with the *Los Angeles Times*. Graciously, make it clear to the interviewer that your time is limited, so when you have finished discussing what you intended to say, you can exit smoothly by asking for just one last question.

If the answer to "How much time do we have?" is always less time than you need to explain, talk, or catch up, you may be talking too much. This is frustrating for both sides of the conversation: the long-winded side because the audience doesn't pay attention and to the short-attention side because there's more talking than interest.

It's important to read your audience members here, too. Do they care about what you are telling them? Or are they just trying to be polite? How do you know? Are they asking questions or shifting in their seats? Looking at you or their watches? Appearing relaxed or gathering their things?

When you are being paid to give a speech or lecture or to conduct a seminar or workshop, someone is always watching the clock for you. Most often, it's a better idea to let an audience out a little early—"Time off for good behavior," I usually tell them—than to drag it out. Someone wise once said, "The human mind can only absorb as long as the butt can sit still."

But to make sure your sponsor is getting his money's worth, announce your availability for private conversation after the audience is excused and stay in the room until the time is up. Sometimes people come back with personal questions even after they've left with their coworkers.

Conversational

The most effective way to plug a product, service, or book is to mention it, by name, in conversation. First, title a book or name your company, product, or service in a way that is easy to include in both written and verbal conversation. For example, "Getting Ready for Media will allow you to," "You're not Ready yet," "When you are Ready for Media interviews," "Being Ready for Media and personal appearances means," "At Ready for Media, we coach you to...." Then practice dropping your mention into conversation easily and naturally, without overdoing it. Twice in a five-minute TV appearance is enough, accompanied by new information that will tweak the audience's interest. Instead of referring to your company as us, we, it, and your product as new and improved, the most technically advanced on the market, or above and beyond the competition, name it as the subject of your sentence. Talk about it by name. Use it as a noun instead of a pronoun. Perhaps, surprisingly, not saying the name you want to promote is the most common mistake businesspeople make in sales, media, and personal appearances as well as events. It's verbal as well as visual signage. For example, "people in business need to know what to say at a moment's notice by learning how to speak off the cuff."

Careful

A sound bite is correctly called "the shot heard round the world." Good or bad, sound bites seem to live forever. And all too often they become their author's personal moniker, tag line, or advertising slogan. And in our fast-paced, information-hungry world, the quotable quote says a lot with a few, well-chosen words. It is a good exercise to sum up the essence of your purpose, your speech, or your mission statement in a sound bite you can deliver, with spontaneity, in a simple sentence or phrase of five to seven seconds.

Candid

Tactful candor and simple honesty is very refreshing in today's world of bluffing and hype. But don't wait until you arrive and are asked a question to decide what you can reveal. Explore with yourself and your company what you are willing to share ahead of time. If you can't give your questioners or interviewers everything, which in most cases you shouldn't, know what you can give them to make a story or anecdote colorful, interesting, and worth listening to or writing about. Because Ready for Media's studio is near Hollywood, we are often asked to coach celebrities who are usually gun-shy about the press. Exploring, in advance, what secrets they feel safe in giving away—adventures from a recent vacation or set location, favorite sports or hobbies, environmental concerns, etc.— is the secret to making them interesting interviewees. Speak to audiences as you would a friend with a big mouth: with careful candor, circumspect trust, and respect.

Cogent

Defined by *Merriam-Webster's Dictionary* as forceful and to the point; compelling, and persuasive. Stephen Covey's *7 Habits of Highly Successful People* includes the practice of beginning with the end in mind. Begin, then, by deciding what opinion you want changed or action you want taken by your presentation, and go for it.

Convincing

Show respect for your audience with a logical presentation. Does it come to a reasonable conclusion? The most compelling speech is one that makes sense. Ask any debater, it isn't the side you're on, but how convincingly you make your case. Does your presentation have structure? Like all good stories, does it have a beginning, middle, and an end?

Confident

There's an old saying in coaching, "Fake it till you make it." Or act "as if" you've had more experience, know-how, or education. Be as prepared and knowledgeable as possible. Then ask yourself, *If not now, then when?* And rise to the occasion. If you are in the position to do something, chances are that you are there for a good reason. Sure, you will do it better next time, but this experience will help ensure that. There's a first time for everything and everyone. Be your own confidence coach. Smile and radiate confidence. Remember that the best defense is a good offense and that, in Hayes's words, "The expert at anything was once a beginner."

Clear

Logical flow can go a long way to making a case. Ask any lawyer. But one person's clarity is another's confusion. So test your logic on friends to make sure it stands up to scrutiny.

Compassionate

Show your passion, compassion, warmth, and humor. Radiate confidence and energy. Use the mantra professed by New York maven Dorothy Sarnoff, "I'm glad I'm here, I'm glad you're here. I know what I know and I care about you."

Cool, Calm, and Collected

Keep your cool. Stay calm and collected. Bottom-line each point, one at a time in a simple sentence. Use your second sentence to trigger the next question.

Correct

It's a fact-checked world, so acknowledge what you know and don't try to answer hypothetical questions. If you are posed one, reject it in favor of the facts as they are known to you. For example, in a press conference, the press corps may ask you to speculate in "what if" scenarios. Resist them and go back to the facts. Avoid beginning your answer with "I," as in, "I don't know" or even "I don't have the answer." It sounds guilty. Begin with any word but "I." Say instead, "The answer isn't clear yet." Acknowledge the question without verifying or admitting to it, then bridge to your answer, which is delivered conversationally.

To be correct, you must be honest. Not only with what is true, but what your audience understands to be true. If you are going to take issue with the audience's understanding, then that is your speech.

Compelling

Does your communication make people care? Do you touch your audience with your voice, your side of things, your predicament, or the audience's? You will know by the audience's reaction and action in response to you and your case for or against something.

Consistent

As a spokesperson for yourself, an issue, or your company, consistency of the message is crucial. And it's not only what you say with words, but with actions, too. Are your habits, behaviors, and conversation consistent with your values? For example, if your word is your bond, how much integrity do you have if you are chronically late? If you value organization, shouldn't it be reflected in a desk that's neat enough to find things?

One company or one voice is more of a challenge when your message reaches around the world. Client companies have taken my communications consulting firm, Ready for Media worldwide from Santa Clara, California, to Tokyo to Munich to Hong Kong and back to make sure that their message rings true for every audience. Singing from the same hymnbook in all of your communications makes you credible.

Credible

You need to be credible and trustworthy, as a company, as a spokesperson and as an individual. Establish your credibility by name-dropping as background. It answers the questions that people are often too intimidated to ask.

Crisis Conscious

In a crisis situation, answer questions with an acknowledgment of compassion, the bottom line in a sound bite, appropriate history, repetition of the sound bite, and the next steps. Sometimes this scenario is repeated over and over again throughout the hours and days of a crisis. It helps to follow this agenda, the details of which you revise as time makes things more clear.

Controversial

The media and their audiences love their bad boys. As John F. Kennedy said, "My experience in government is that when things are non-controversial, beautifully coordinated and all the rest, it must be because there is not much going on."

So, if controversy serves your purpose, use it. Remember, though, that you are not the only one who should be served.

Audiences quickly tire of outspoken spokespeople who take a self-serving approach and are merely in it for themselves.

Charismatic

Gifted with God's grace or favor, Charisma is an elusive butterfly that's hard to define but you know it when you find it. It may simply be the quality that makes everyone feel good about about being themselves.

According to *Merriam-Webster's Dictionary*, charisma comes from the Greek words *charis* ("grace, beauty, kindness") and *charizesthai* ("to show favor to"). It's defined as a divinely inspired gift, grace, or talent; a special quality of leadership that captures the popular imagination and inspires unswerving allegiance and devotion. It's been my experience that charismatic people are also funny, generous, kind, and compassionate for the human condition.

One of the nation's most charismatic presidents, John F. Kennedy, quoted Francis Bacon in an address to a White House dinner and reception honoring Nobel Prize winners in April of 1962: "In a time of turbulence and change, it is more true than ever that knowledge is power." In referring to his audience of honorees, the president went on to say, "I think this is the most extraordinary collection of talent, of human knowledge, that has ever been gathered together at the White House, with the possible exception of when Thomas Jefferson dined alone."

One of the most charismatic women I know has a habit of making everyone feel important and valued. And she is selective. She knows that she can't be all things to all people, so she chooses carefully who does the most for her, too. She shares some of her personality with everyone she knows and is adored by the people who work for her.

From the handshake to handing over your business card, don't look for the whites of their eyes, but look at the color.

Once you've registered the color of the eyes that are being introduced to you, you've kept enough direct eye contact to be considered charismatic. U.S. presidents Bill Clinton and George W. Bush are legendary for this skill.

Because communication is the third C after chemistry and compatibility in any relationship, it should not surprise you that establishing a command of all the Cs will change your relationships and the life that you build around them.

Mastering the Moment

Men flourish only for a moment.

—Homer

When you are standing before hundreds of people or find yourself Facing the Nation or Meeting the Press, who among us doesn't feel the tug of personal destiny? Is there anyone who doesn't hope and pray to...

Master the Moment

Yet often we do not, and it is more than a matter of charisma; for even the best speakers flop now and then. What keeps them in the limelight is that they so seldom fail at what they do best: gain and retain audience interest, sometimes under intense conditions. Imagine the pressure on an evangelist, minister, or president facing the flock during a breaking sex scandal.

A good dollop of charisma would help, of course, yet that's not what survivors such as Jane Fonda or Bill Clinton depend on. Newsmakers and leaders have mastered many moments. They've made their missteps and lived to tell about them.

As masters of their own destiny, they know all too well that to do well up front, you must be prepared to *be* up front. Integrity and authenticity go a long way in establishing your credibility, because the lens doesn't lie, whether it is in the eyes of your audience or on the front of a camera.

Lee Iacocca said that being honest is the best foundation—to be clear and candid about what must be accomplished and what sacrifices may be involved. And in the case of a serious problem, you cannot do much to put out a brush fire if you first insist there isn't one.

If you are constantly putting out fires instead of fireproofing, there will be no chance to take the second step and...

Master the Method

If you are in a relatively formal role in your professional life, trying to be folksy on a platform can be risky. You can also be a fish out of water if you are naturally casual and try to be formal because this is an "important" occasion. If no one ever laughs at your jokes, don't try to reverse the trend while standing before an audience.

If you don't know what people love about you, find out, and be genuine. Be yourself—and be the best you can be at being you.

Master the Medium

Third, be a master of your *medium*. Know what presentation media you'll be using and how to handle it well.

Go to the speech site days before and be very early on the day of the event to get the lay of the land and take care of logistics.

I was once a perfect lady, following tradition and waiting for the president of a men's club to escort me to the speaker's table for a breakfast and speech (mine) before hundreds of invited guests. Imagine my surprise, and theirs, when the monitors that were to provide video examples for my speech projected only noise. Despite technicians crawling under the table to fix things as I spoke, the noise, not the pictures, continued throughout the speech.

Because you will be the one who looks bad when the monitor doesn't work, a microphone doesn't project, or a podium light flickers, don't leave anything to chance or to somebody else. And even in today's high-tech world, it is better to use an old-fashioned slide projector/remote changer or even an overhead with ease than to fumble with a computer-based presentation you don't know how to operate.

If your medium is the media, know the rules and how to play the game—proactively. Offer to be a media resource as an expert in your field. Cultivate media contacts and beat reporters in your industry by genuinely complimenting them on a well-researched story. Put a press release out over the wires with sound statistics or new information. Make yourself available for background or a sound bite when there's a breaking story.

To be truly successful in mastering the moment, you must also...

Master the Material

To be truly successful in mastering the moment, you must be a master of your *material,* which means more than just the technical knowledge. You must be able to adapt it to the

level of the audience and have it organized in a way that will
lead your audience to respond. The material should be second
nature to you, allowing you the freedom to work the room and
an audience. Professional athletes practice for hours shooting
free throws, making putts, or hitting against a backboard. Then,
when the game begins, they can simply play. In a stand-up
presentation, you must be able to marshal facts or processes,
and to do so in a way that makes them both clear and useful. If
nothing else, you will be prepared for the unexpected.

I once flew to Chicago from Los Angeles for a new business presentation, only to find my audience rushing past me to
the airport to fly in the company jet to the site of a crisis. "Come
with us," they said, "to see how things really happen around
here and you can give us your pitch on the way." I went, I saw,
I got the client.

Fellow writer Tom Snyder holds a doctorate, with a specialty in small-group communication and systems analysis. He
was scheduled to lead an interactive session for top executives
wrestling with integrating new digital solutions to management
issues. There was a crisis when he arrived, however, and no
management team members were available. Having scheduled and paid for his time, the company brought in telephone
operators instead of managers. "Happily," Tom says, "my own
training had been so rigorous that it was a case of adapting
group processes to meet communications issues. At the end of
the day, the phone operators had a proposal for management
that would save money and ease their workload."

Finally, you must...

Master the Message

Master the *message* by keeping whatever you are presenting simple and organized around a single idea, preferably a
provocative, profound, or at least cogent thought, to make it

worth the audience's time. As I put it to clients, "What's the point?" Presentations with several competing ideas only compete for the attention of an audience that is no longer clear about what is important.

Three to five single sub-points may be used to support that one idea, but be sure that one main idea or message is clearly and concisely presented. If the angle were to be written up as a magazine or news story, what would be the headline? At the end of your presentation, the audience must know and be able to say exactly what your presentation was about and what they learned from you.

And as you are sifting through facts or a process you intend to present, remember that a spoonful of sugar makes the medicine go down. Don't let the facts be dull and repetitious. Informing is only part of your job. The rest is to enlighten, perhaps entertain, and certainly to inspire.

When you know what you are presenting well enough, you are then able to make contact with your audience on an individual level. Notice how great performers always seem to be singing to one person? That's because they are—one and then another, then another. To be interesting to your audience, you must be interested *in* your audience. The magic of a meeting is in consensus; the magic of a stand-up program lies with acceptance. In both cases, individuals begin to respond as part of a group, with you as their leader, the master of the moment.

Business Etiquette

*Each of us is constantly marketing ourselves
for success or failure depending on our
behavior, manners and mannerisms, habits,
business protocol and personal etiquette.*

—W. Henry Walker,
Farmers & Merchants Bank

Arrogance, which *Merriam-Webster's Dictionary* defines as "the state of being arrogant; full of unwarranted pride and self-importance; overbearing; haughty," seems to be the behavior least admired in leaders and would-be leaders. Recent history is littered with bodies that were brought down for lack of humility. Sadly, it almost always seems to be a front that masks an otherwise poor self-image. It inspires followers to root and, sometimes even vote, for a downfall, or at least a comeuppance. Painful comeuppances.

A September 22, 2003, *BusinessWeek* article titled "What's an MBA Really Worth?" concluded that after 10 years, most alums of the prestigious business schools—men and women alike—have

> [F]ound their way to the upper echelons of management, but not without some painful comeuppances along the way. Marching into jobs as smug know-it-alls, they soon found out that "you don't just step into a CEO role after two years of business schools," reported MIT's Sloan School of Management alum Richard Wong, now senior vice-president of marketing at Openwave Systems Inc. "What some people don't realize [when they graduate] is that being a top manager is an earned right."

Further, the loudest complaint of the mostly Ivy League educated MBAs was about just how ill-prepared alums felt when faced with the office politics and challenges of "managing in the middle." Many report that they should have been required to take more organization behavior classes, "though it's like trying to get someone to eat their spinach," conceded 40-year-old Charles W. Breer, a Big 10 University of Michigan business school graduate who has spent most of his post-MBA career working for Northwest Airlines Corp. "Still, actual office politics—the tricky mix of sociology, personality and corporate culture that exists in every workplace—can make a mockery of B-school theory. Breer says his hardest times were managing a 12-person staff. 'At a minimum, I wish someone had told me this would be one of the biggest challenges, and then given me some tips,' says Breer."

As one of Ready for Media's current clients puts it: "How important is what you do if you can't conduct yourself properly while you do it?"

Shaking Hands

As a rule, Europeans shake hands for everything, air kiss both sides of the face, and men hug other men. America refers back to its less touchy, Puritan origins and, in business, favors a simple handshake—not pulverizing, but firm. It's best to save the two-hand handshake and air kiss for personal encounters or old friends.

An executive may reach over and shake hands from behind his or her desk, but it is thought to be more gracious and welcoming when he or she comes around to greet the visitor. Appropriate greetings include "I am pleased to meet you" and "How do you do?" reinforced by a sincere smile and direct eye contact.

Networking

Mixers and cocktail parties were invented before networking was, with its requirements of shaking hands, presenting cards, and making notes. How does one graciously maneuver a glass and an hors d'oeuvre plate at the same time? Never just stand at a buffet table and shovel or, heaven forbid, go back into a dip after you've taken a bite out of the chip, carrot, shrimp, or whatever!

My secret is to secure the stem of the wine glass with my thumb on the plate or hold the tumbler-shaped glass with the plate in the left hand, leaving the other free to fill the plate (judiciously) eat, drink, shake hands, and pull cards from a pocket. The practice Scarlett O'Hara pioneered in *Gone With the Wind* of eating at home before the party is a good one, although not always practical with today's schedules, traffic, and geography. Not only would that free your hands from eating, it would ensure that you eat before you drink. It is nutritional as well as social suicide to skip breakfast and lunch, and then try to make up for it with last-minute hors d'oeuvres or drink on an empty stomach.

Working a room may be a mystery to at least two generations who have grown up in front of television and computer screens. Never leaving our rooms long enough to go to a cotillion or even to have dinner with Mom and Dad may mean that we do not have the social skills or table manners to meet and greet potential clients, dine with the boss's wife, or work a trade show.

Increasingly, companies are requesting business and social etiquette coaching for their young and new hires as well as potential executives whose manners may be lacking.

The vice president of a major financial firm confided to me, "Our young financial advisors almost always know more than the clients about investing, but a sophisticated, worldly client doesn't want to invest their time or money with young men or women whose grammar or etiquette suggests that they are not savvy enough to manage money."

Ready for Media's textbook client in the 20th century was the brilliant college dropout who had begun the technology boom in his garage and had lots of media interest in himself and his 3- to 5-year-old $100 million public company. This century's clients are bright MBAs, PhDs, Esquires, and all the rest who can't make it through a client meeting or business dinner with out faux pas. Their bosses are gold-standard clients who are the successful, entrepreneurial, Ivy League–educated leaders of both public and private companies as well as law firms who want polish and propriety for them.

Table manners, grooming, and punctuality won't make, but can surely break, a power breakfast or business dinner.

Table Manners

A simple rule of thumb is to follow the lead of the host or most distinguished person at the table. Remember that the meal and drinks are actually secondary to the social interaction or conversation. *Do* make your menu choices similar to the host's, decide quickly, and ask that things be passed to you instead of making a boarder house reach across the table. *Don't* shovel food, talk with your mouth full, taste another's food, begin to eat until everyone is served, or drink more than one glass of anything with alcohol. Invite the host or hostess to order first and then match it as closely as you can in price, complexity, and detail, allowing for your own individual limitations.

As the host or hostess, be gracious by making everyone feel welcome and entirely appropriate. There is a favorite story, whether true or not, that the Duchess of Windsor, a very fine hostess, once took her cues from a boorish guest of honor and all of her other guests followed suit so she could make the stranger feel totally appropriate and at home. The moral is "When you know the rules, you can break them." Otherwise, it's just plain ignorance.

Wardrobe and Grooming

Even in the world of business casual, the manner in which you dress is not only an indicator of your rank today, but also of your future. As much as possible, dress for the position you want to move into. And only impeccable grooming will do.

I'm often asked about facial hair such as beards and mustaches. Look around; it's mostly the look for artists, professors, students, and techies—not for those in the corporate suites. The same can be said for combovers. Today's very close cropped hair or shaved head for a balding man is the perfect solution to an inevitable situation for many.

The Early Bird

The early bird gets the worm, as they say! So be on time or, better yet, a little early. There is a surprising sense of power and control when you are the one who is waiting for the others rather than rushing in at the last minute full of apology and not knowing what you've missed.

Small Talk

Small talk is a big subject. Where do you start? What's appropriate? What's not? How long do you engage in it before transitioning to your reason for the meeting? Who makes the transition? Is it worse to talk too much or too little?

Opening topics are typically the venue, the occasion, the weather, the traffic, sports, even the news if it's not too political or gruesome. You are looking for commonalities. Areas in which you can agree or have similar experiences. Do your research ahead of time and know as much as possible about the person or people you will be meeting. Never go into a meeting, job interview, or event without having read that morning's newspapers. It never fails that the person with whom you are meeting's company or industry will be on the business pages and you want to know about it before you get there.

Ahead of time, request biographical information from assistants or "Google" the people you'll be meeting to get a leg up on where they went to college or grad school, their interests and hobbies, what boards they belong to, etc. Your job is to get them talking about their favorite subjects, experiences, and ideas. Be a good listener. Ask thoughtful questions. People like to learn from conversations, and if they can learn from your interest in them, so much the better!

No scripts here, but keep your head about you. What you say and how you say it will have a lot to do with how you and your company are perceived. So edit yourself and think before you speak. Avoid slang, swear words, or expressions that typecast you. Imagine the reaction of customers to a beautiful but naïve young lady who was in the habit of proclaiming, "Holy sh*t!" every time something surprised her.

Trade Shows

For the sake of efficiency, companies use industry trade shows and association events as opportunities to showcase or sell new products to the trade, and as client or professional interface and networking opportunities.

If you are a "booth sitter," you are the greeter and gracious host. Welcome all visitors to your booth and product demonstrations with a smile and an offer to be of assistance. Your friendly personality will put a face and a name on your product line and company in customers' or potential customers' minds. So put yourself out to enhance the major investment the company has made in your being at the show.

However, your willingness to help should be in *finding* rather than *being* the media spokesperson who talks to the press, unless you are specifically coached to do so. Instead, facilitate media coverage for your company by knowing who the designated hitters are and offering to introduce them and provide their contact information through business cards.

Talking to the media without being ready for it is playing with fire. Don't spoil years of hard work getting ahead in your company and career by letting your name be attached to a sound bite heard round the world, industry, and company. I can't forget, or forgive, the forest products company employee who was quoted by the press as voluntarily saying, "If that means cutting a 14-*foot* (diameter) Sequoia, that's reasonable to prevent (forest) fire." The next day's Associated Press retraction that he actually said cutting a 14-*inch* (diameter) only repeated the injury and the insult. Although the word *cutting* is common in his industry, to choose it for public consumption in the same sentence as Sequoia only fueled the fire of his outraged and indignant environmental opponents.

In this Age of the Sound Bite, what you say is every bit as important as how you say it. Probably more so because the words will be quoted out of context, usually in print and by others without the inflection or meaning that you perhaps intended. I remember years ago how important it was in coaching the Canadian Ambassador, who was in Los Angeles for a popular radio talk-show to use the word *harvesting* instead of his environmental opponents' phrase of *slaughtering* baby seals. The truth was that the animals were farmed just like chickens, hogs, and beef cattle to provide food, clothing, and other necessities of human life. And I taught him to say so.

The reason that environmentalists often seem to win in the media's court of public opinion is their obvious passion for their cause. In an effort to be *professional*, too many equally caring and concerned businesspeople forget to show their passion in the name of purpose.

Association Mixers, Cocktail Parties, and Networking Events

If these events remind you that you were a wallflower in high school and nothing has changed, here are some tips:

- Arrive early, before the cliques are formed and begin your own conversation with new people as they arrive, informally playing the role of hostess or greeter.
- Include others in your conversation to give them a sense of comfort and gratitude.
- Find or create an unofficial role for yourself (name-card maker, guest-list monitor, pollster) that gives you an ice-breaker.
- Open a conversation with a genuine compliment that is appropriate for a business, rather than personal situation.

In other than business casual situations, men's ties and women's jewelry are still their personal statements and thus, are usually a safe area for compliments. Avoid commenting on other items of clothing, hair, or eye color, particularly if you are of the opposite sex. It seems too personal and may be read as an inappropriate flirtation.

It seems a small thing, but there is a right and a wrong side for your name tag. Put it on your right side, so the people you meet can see your name and your company, written legibly, when they shake hands with you.

Usually, at events held in the United States, business cards are not exchanged until the end of the conversation and then only if the conversation has created a reason to stay in touch. By that time, everyone has pretty much forgotten each other's name and exact title, so the business card is a good reminder.

It is good etiquette to ask for another's business card before presenting yours. It also puts you in the power position to have his or her contact information to continue the business relationship. In the United States, it is perfectly acceptable, and even recommended, to note on the back of another's business card the date and place of the meeting and the action steps for following up with a good contact.

However, don't do this in Japan! Observe the Japanese practice of treating a business card with utmost respect by not writing on it or shoving it into a wallet or card case. Rather, accept it with both hands in a manner similar to its presentation and politely comment on some information on the card. At table meetings, the hierarchical Japanese have taught us to exchange cards upon first meeting and to keep them in front of us as a reference for name and rank throughout the meeting.

More Cultural Differences

In communications that span different cultures, mannerisms are important, too. When people from my company coach Asian clients to meet Westerners, we always have to assist the

Asian executives in making direct eye contact and strengthening the firmness of their handshakes. Conversely, expect a very gentle or seemingly wimpy connection when you shake hands with Asians, particularly the women.

In the United States, anything other than direct eye contact makes a person seem shifty-eyed or even guilty. The open, direct gaze that we favor often seems too confrontational to Asian executives. My favorite public relations executive in Tokyo is extremely deferential, even stand-offish, to his Japanese woman client so as not to offend her.

For the most part, people from western Europe expect dinner-table conversation to be about art, literature, even sports, but not business. Whereas the values Americans live by include a strong work ethic—isn't business why we have a business dinner anyway?

Tailor your practice to the culture and country in which you find yourself. In short, the American can seem very much the bull in the china shop when doing business in these cultures. Practicing a "less is more" approach is wise and prudent to creating a good business environment.

Thank You Notes

Saying a few words in a thank you note after a job interview or other first meeting makes a very good impression. Simply acknowledge your appreciation for the opportunity to meet him or her in person, talk about _____, and your anticipation of the next steps.

Your choice in personal stationery need not be expensive, but should look as professional as possible. A simple white or ecru card or folded card with a border and matching envelope is very appropriate. The stationery can be personalized with your initials embossed or engraved in a dignified and tailored style but isn't necessary. Write in blue or black ink and affix with a stamp that is appropriately dignified, as well.

The best etiquette is following a version of the Golden Rule, do unto others as they would have you do unto them.

Beginnings and Endings

Whatever you do or dream, begin it.
For boldness has power, magic and even
genius in it.

—Johann Wolfgang von Goethe,
German philosopher

The most important moments of your presentation are the first and last ones. Everything else may be forgotten if it starts or ends badly. Audiences decide on you as a presenter just as they do when meeting you in person—within minutes. And you don't get a second chance to make that first impression.

Usually the best attention-getting beginnings come out of real-life experiences that are funny or insightful.

One personal experience that made a memorable beginning came from a very young-looking ophthalmologist planning a speech to the senior citizens he hoped to recruit as cataract patients. To establish credibility, I coached him to start by telling his own story. That day, an aging audience learned that my client wanted to be an eye doctor ever since the summer he spent temporarily blinded by a pop fly in a Little League game. That's when he had promised God that if he could ever see again, he would help others see, too. His pact with God still goes a long way in establishing credibility with an elderly audience.

Finding Your Audience

Research has proven that in a speech, until you have built rapport, captured attention, headlined the speech, explained its value, and established your credentials, you don't even *have* an audience.

Begin the creation process of speech writing by asking yourself who the audience is and why what you have to say is important to them. No kidding. Right up front, you should tell them why this is important for them and why they are important to you. Then fill in the blanks, "As _____ (stockholders, readers, middle managers, decision-makers, voters, or moms and dads) it's important that you _____." This reminds you, too, that something must be accomplished here. Even though you've probably already been introduced, the audience may not have paid much attention before you had their attention. Your credentials are not just an abriged version of your resume, they highlight something that makes your background particularly appropriate in this situation. What from your experience can you open with to get their attention? Let the moral of that story be the main point, headline, or title of the speech.

The philosophy behind this is that you can't really begin until you have the audience's attention, they know the point, they understand what's in it for them, and what qualifies you to be their leader, in this venture at least.

Even before the attention-getter, some speakers opt for a rapport-builder. Former president Lyndon Johnson would often warm up an audience by acknowledging his introduction in a way that everyone could relate to, "That was the kind of very generous introduction my father would have appreciated and my mother would have believed." Vice President Walter Mondale was a little less flattered, "Of all the introductions I have ever received, that was the most recent."

In a recent presentation to an audience of public relations professionals, I mentioned an interview on the economy from the previous night with George Bush by CNBC's Ron Insana. I explained that Ron had once worked with me on coaching executives for financial interviews and that having journalists with such distinguished credentials was important in media coaching. "Experience teaches" was my moral, or main point. "Protecting your media contacts by making sure your clients approach the media successfully is why media coaching is important," I explained. My credentials included my own background as a journalist, including as a print reporter, which broadens my coaching ability even further.

I included three sub-points on how to choose a media strategy and coaching firm, and then I headlined, detailed, and reviewed each one before repeating the main point. Ask yourself what additional points you're going to tell them (preview), tell them (view), and then tell them that you told them (review). Finally, what thought or message must I leave with my audience? In my case, "Experience teaches best."

What About Jokes?

Opening with a joke is very risky, unless it is brilliant and perfectly appropriate for the audience and occasion. After 9/11, comedian Ellen DeGeneres opened the twice-canceled Emmy Awards with, "This ought to make the Taliban really crazy: a gay woman in a suit surrounded by Jews!"

It was brilliant not only for the audience, but for Ellen. Humor can backfire unless it is very appropriate to the situation. Almost without exception, jokes about an ethnic group are unacceptable (even blondes get offended) unless the speaker is clearly one of them. Comedians don't read jokes, they practice telling them to anyone and everyone who will listen: themselves, the mirror, the video camera, the dog, their mothers, and the baby. And everywhere they can: the shower, the car, the treadmill, or the driving range. Bore your friends and your family, not your audience.

Don't test it on anyone who's going to be in the audience, they might tell it first and give your punch line away. Choose someone you can count on to be a tough critic, someone who won't pull punches, and someone who'll tell you that it doesn't work.

Short, true-life stories with humor, paradox, or pathos are usually safer, even for professional comedians.

I'll never forget the time the program chair introduced a panel on the subject "Trust in Trying Times." The panelists were a group of public relations professionals who had been through the corporate scandals and stock dalliances of their respective corporations. She began by telling the story of the donkey that had fallen into a well and no matter how he screamed or squirmed, the farmer couldn't get him out. To put the poor animal out of his misery, the farmer and all the neighbors took shovels full of dirt and poured them down the well. Surprised to see the dirt coming, the donkey shook each shovelful from his back to the ground and stepped on it. After a time, the well filled up and the donkey stepped out of the well and ran off. It was the perfect story because despite all the dirt that had been shoveled at these corporate public relations people, they had lived to tell about it.

Something happens to an audience when it knows there's a joke or punch line coming. People seem to relax. They can have fun before they have to start paying attention and learn something. Linus Pauling's philosophy that laughter is the best medicine is at play here. So, look for an *appropriate* joke, story, or moral to relax your audience from the start.

Unfortunately, the program chair didn't know when to stop and reduced her own moral by saying that the donkey came back and did the farmer and all the neighbors in, which is what happens when you try to cover your ass.

Beginning Questions

One way to open a speech is to ask the audience at the beginning what they hope to learn about the subject. One at a time, audience members raise their hands, asking the questions that they usually have to save for the end. The element of surprise can be a great attention-getter and actually helps the speaker tailor his or her remarks to the announced interest of the audience.

The danger of this approach, of course, is that if the questions are entirely out of left field, the speaker's prepared remarks may seem irrelevant. One speaker, very experienced with his subject, added to the attention-getting by good-naturedly wadding up the paper with his prepared remarks and tossing it away. "Okay, then," he said with a laugh. "Let's talk about what you want to talk about."

It did intrigue the audience with what they were missing and he knew his subject well enough that he eventually included everything, but in a customized way.

If you need, as most of us do, your prepared speech for security and talking points, you may want to phrase your opening question this way: "One of my favorite T-shirts reads 'Life Is Short, Eat Dessert First.' Because "dessert" in after-dinner speeches is usually the questions and answers, let's start with those so I'll make sure to *include* what you came to hear."

This technique allows you to give the entire audience the impression that you have listened to them before speaking. If you ask them to say their names along with their questions, you can reference them by name when you get to the pertinent points they've asked about.

Avoid this technique, though, if you suspect a hostile audience or one that may have competitors who would take the floor and your time to grandstand.

Other Beginnings

Another speaker began her speech by arranging her cell phone to ring the minute she arrived at the podium. She pretended to answer it and used the phone to begin the speech on Technology: Tools of the Future.

Skits *can* backfire, however. Once, in the name of attention-getting, my colleagues and I began a speech with a sales scenario where everything was done wrong but we failed to tell the audience what we were doing. Our audience was a group of take-no-prisoners salespeople—some got it, but most didn't. We lost our credibility from the start and never got it back.

Another speaker on time management failed to tell the audience that he was merely pretending to be disheveled and disorganized at the beginning of his speech in order to make the point that disorganization wastes time, energy, and focus. He never got another chance to make an organized first impression.

I once started an afternoon conference workshop about 10 or 15 minutes late. Trying to be cool, I failed to mention that my tardiness was a result of my morning flight to the city being canceled due to weather and then taking heroic measures to fly to a nearby city, rent a car, and drive through a torrential rainstorm to make the event at all!

To me, and the organizers, it seemed a miracle that I was even there. Many of the presenters didn't make it. But by failing to acknowledge or explain what I'd done to be with them, several in my audience thought I was rude to begin late and said so in their presenter evaluations. That means they harbored negative feelings throughout the afternoon and nothing I did altered that first impression.

If I could do it again, I would use the hours spent driving to craft the experience into a beginning rapport-builder that would lead to my subject. Perhaps, "Communication at all costs," or "Neither snow, nor rain, nor heat, nor gloom of night stays these couriers from the swift completion of their appointed rounds," as the New York City Post Office inscription reads.

Stuff happens. Ambulances roar by at funerals. Cell phones ring unexpectedly. The electricity goes out so that video playback monitors that you've rehearsed with for hours don't work. Despite everyone's best efforts, even the founders of giant technology companies have experienced technical meltdowns in front of huge audiences at computer trade shows.

The speakers who can be humorous and roll with the punches because they are relaxed enough to be spontaneous are the ones who triumph over adversity and win the appreciation and approval of their audiences.

Ending Questions

One of the most terrifying moments of any speech is when you ask if there are any questions, and there are none. You've probably left a third to a half of your time for questions and no one speaks up. You may have just answered all of the questions in a really complete speech or the audience members may be shy or intimidated by their peers. But it gives the impression that no one is, or was, really interested.

Solution: Bring three or four really good questions (ones you have answers for) with you along with extra information that hasn't been covered in the prepared remarks. Then pose them to the audience with, "You might be asking yourself..." or "You may be wondering...," then answer them. This may serve to prime the pump and get them started asking their own questions or may simply finish your presentation smoothly.

Both at the beginning and end, you can use questions to your advantage as a speaker.

Completing the Circle

Revisit the beginning at the end. If you began with a story, tell the audience how it came out at the end. If your main point was a quote, restate it with emphasis or a twist. "Familiarity breeds contempt" was the moral from the Aesop's fable *The Fox and the Lion*. To which Mark Twain added, "Familiarity breeds contempt—and children." The classic martini, with a twist!

Begin, and end, on time. Or better yet, end a little early. Even if you are a paid speaker and want to impress the organizers so they know they've gotten their money's worth, stop yourself with a particularly good answer a few minutes before you have to. In today's over-booked society, nothing is more appreciated than the gift of a little found time.

According to Ronald Reagan's speechwriter, Peggy Noonan, he believed that no one wants to sit in an audience in respectful silence for more than 20 minutes. Then, offer up to 20 minutes of Q&A and everyone gets to go home!

Nothing is worse than keeping an audience trapped into the night. Don't fall in love with the sound of your own words. You will undo all the good you've done by dragging it out to get in just one more point. By finishing a bit early, you leave everything and everyone on a positive note, hopefully wanting more for the next time.

The Greek playwright Euripides is credited with the pithy observation that "a bad beginning makes a bad ending." I would add that a bad or weak ending makes a bad beginning for the next time and sends everyone, including the speaker, home with a feeling of disappointment of what could have been that wasn't. One of the best things about the trepidation that often accompanies public speaking is the adrenalin or natural high that comes with it. Most speakers I know need to wind down after the excitement of any personal appearance.

The end of a speech requires three things: (1) a payoff or something dramatic (but not necessarily forceful) , (2) a sense of humility, and (3) a reiteration of expectations or call to action. A movie isn't over until it has delivered on the promise, and a sales call isn't finished until you've asked for the order.

Using, but not overusing, quotes also helps allay the fear of not knowing where to begin or end. Both *Bartlett's Familiar Quotations* and search-engine quotation Web pages are organized by subject. So, with simply an idea of what the audience needs from you, you can begin to build your message around the profound words others have used.

When in Rome

The rain in Spain stays mainly in the plain.

—My Fair Lady

I haven't been to Rome yet. Or Tuscany. In fact, I haven't been to Italy at all. But I have traveled in Paris, Hong Kong, Munich, Tokyo, London, and Montreal, where I've solicited a media interview or two. And even though I don't always speak the language, I do my best to be as appropriately attuned to the cultures and practices as possible. In general, follow these conventions:

- In Italy (where the paparazzi got their name) remember that media coverage is often a circus.
- In Asia, remember that "Orientals" are rugs, the people are Asian.
- In Japan, treat business cards with respect by presenting them with both hands and not marking, folding, or stuffing them in a pocket.

- In Beijing, be sensitive to the politics.
- In Vietnam, remember that money talks.
- In Taipei, Hong Kong, and China, be respectful of elders and authority.
- In Germany, be direct, clear, and concise.
- In Switzerland, be charming and gracious.
- In London, dress conservatively.
- In Ireland, show fairness.
- In England, be thick-skinned. The tabloids can be scathing.
- In Scandinavia, don't be prudish.
- In Russia, show respect for the Church.
- In New Zealand, be down to earth, not fancy, and glib or overly slick.
- In Hawaii, wear shoes and socks if you mean business.
- In Honolulu, choose the most expensive and tasteful Hawaiian shirt for most business meetings.
- In Toronto, let your sophistication show.
- In Brazil, focus on lifestyles.
- In South and Latin America, grandstand.
- In the United States, be honest. Make direct eye contact. Don't lie, mislead, or try to bluff. Avoid bribery at all costs. Acknowledge wrongdoing and apologize. Come clean, fall on your sword. Move on.
- In Paris, remember that the French are even more nationalistic than Americans.

That said, my first experience in Paris was far different from that of many of my friends. I'm convinced that it was because I continually started conversations with my best, in fact *only*, French phrase, "Parlez-vous Anglais?"

"Do you speak English?" I more or less pleaded with a helpless smile. It was certainly an appropriate question, and perhaps by not assuming that they would or should speak English just because I was an American gracing their French-speaking country with my presence, everyone was very accommodating. In a world, certainly a business one, where American English is more and more the standard, French is becoming an even more endangered species and is therefore held more dear and defensively by its native speakers. In France and the French-speaking city of Quebec, there is also a strong nationalistic pride in their centuries-old traditions, culture, and history.

My question provided the obvious benefit of speaking their English rather than my French in touring Paris, Lyon, Limoges, Dijon, Aix-en-Provence, and a few natives actually admitted that they enjoyed practicing their English on tourists!

Corporate Culture

The main guideline for Americans traveling to or working in France, besides an appreciation and command of the language, is that you invest time in building relationships.

In general, the French not only speak a romance language but also have a circular or feminine approach versus an American's linear or masculine-directed culture. The image of climbing a corporate ladder is a far cry from building a web or network of relationships in which to do business. Unlike America, where business drives the relationship, the relationship drives the business in France.

This basic difference is also seen in the overlap in a French corporate culture versus the hierarchal stepladder of American's organizational charts where the lines, or boxes, are finely drawn. As Americans, we seem to value our solitude and individual space or cubicle versus the power-sharing, familial approach of the French.

Secondly, if you are working in France, it's important to know and take an active role in the French decision-making process that not only seems to require debate and argument, but often begins from a neutral or negative premise. Conversely, Americans can gush enthusiasm for a project or idea at the beginning, but the Frenchman soon learns that there is almost always another shoe to drop in our "yes, but" style. Additionally, an American executive's eagerness to work things out as she goes is in direct contrast to a French madame's tendency to map the whole thing out before starting. The American is focused on the beginning, the French on the ending.

Time management is a cultural phenomenon that needs a better understanding by both sides as well. American business is dictated by external forces such as calendars and the clock. French workers are guided more by an internal sense of time and organization.

Original Spin-Doctors

A very charming, young Frenchman I know delights his Japanese hosts with his European ways, but in a more self-effacing and humorous than arrogant way. In working for both U.S. and Japanese companies, he has observed vast differences in corporate cultures:

> The U.S. guys are very direct while the Japanese are the total opposite...which sometimes frustrates the Americans and embarrasses and dismays the Japanese. The original spin-doctors, the Japanese don't like to give bad news, especially protecting the hierarchy, so they spin, even internally. As an international player, you must be aware of this spin factor. If you are told, "we'll consider that," by a Japanese manager, it may well mean "no, not ever."

On the other hand, a Japanese client surprised me with his sense of humor and willingness for constructive critique. But in classic Japanese fashion, his lieutenants did not relax and enjoy themselves until their leader indicated his enjoyment of the process and his openness to self-improvement.

Another difference I've noticed among my Japanese clients is that the executives always put themselves through coaching first as a test of the benefits before expecting their direct reports to follow suit. Conversely, American executives are much more likely to let their lieutenants be the guinea pigs in testing a new idea or process before they risk it or take the time themselves.

Experience Teaches

Doing business abroad, whether based there or traveling, is one of the most broadening experiences any employer or client can give you.

In both speaking and writing, communicating with people for whom English is a second language requires thoughtfulness and patience. Consider how much trouble you would have trying to speak in someone else's native tongue. Avoid idioms, acronyms, jargon, and slang. Instead, choose words and phrases where the words actually mean what they say.

Another favorite client of mine is a Brit who is living and working in Munich, Germany, for an American company. His genuine love for his adopted country must be apparent to his hosts, because he is enthusiastically embraced as a manager. Not unlike the southern half of most countries and states in the Northern Hemisphere, the lifestyle and business atmosphere of Munich is more laid back, more friendly than in Berlin.

People seem to reflect the warmth of the cities nearer the equator. They often display a more relaxed attitude than their northern neighbors. For example, examine Munich versus Berlin, Caan versus Paris, San Diego versus San Francisco, and Houston versus Dallas.

That said, one might think that an Italian visitor who was trading her 200-year-old restored Tuscan farmhouse for a Malibu beach house, both from southern climes, might have been welcomed with champagne, a party, or at least open arms. But don't forget that the United States has become a very litigious society and instead, the poor Italian was greeted with a contract to sign, guaranteeing that both damage and injury would be covered by the visitor.

Another phrase I've learned from the French is "Vive la difference!"

What to Say

8

Having a speech writer would be too phony. I just try to remember six words before every talk.

—Mark Spitz, Olympic gold medalist swimmer

Mr. Spitz had the right idea, but once the words are out of your mouth, you can't get them back. Unlike the written word, the spoken word is often said before you think. So, it's always a good idea to have a few logical sound bites in mind when you go into any situation, especially where you could be quoted.

I've had lots of experience coaching Olympic gold medalists from Summer Sanders to twins Karen and Sarah Josephson to America's bobsled team. These professionally trained athletes take direction well and are a gold mine to corporate sponsors. Summer Sanders introduced the blue M&M for M&M Mars, and before the synchronized swim team spelled out VISA

for that commercial sponsor, they had the opportunity to represent Max Factor Waterproof Mascara. It's not a natural thing
when you've just won the Olympic gold and are asked all the
questions about how it feels to win, to mention that, thankfully,
your Max Factor Waterproof Mascara didn't run either in the
pool or now that you are crying tears of joy! But they did.

For the most part, audiences will forgive a commercial
mention if they are getting enough of the information they tuned
in for. Tennis great Arthur Ash was legendary as a spokesperson for aspirin. He became a master at speaking about the
heart-healthy benefits of an aspirin a day during a discussion of
his tennis game.

One of the biggest challenges for celebrities and everyone
who gets interviewed is having something interesting to say.
Often, the questions you are asked are not what you want to
talk about. But there's almost always a way to address the
question with answers that you know will at least interest, if not
directly answer, a reporter and his or her audience.

Part of my job description as an associate producer for
Regis Philbin, before he made millionaires, was to explore with
celebrities and personalities what they were willing to share
with their audiences. What did she like about a co-star? What
was the funniest thing that happened to him on a recent vacation? Why did a particular movie role appeal to him? What was
her secret to anything?

The secret I teach clients is to acknowledge questions
instead of answering them. Then bridge to ready answers
that are safe but are more interesting and sometimes, even
entertaining.

Watch the pros in interviews and on talk shows. A well-
known actress, who naturally didn't want to talk about her pend-
ing divorce from a well-known co-star, did have to talk about her
new movie. We explored interesting facts about her role requir-
ing a vigorous work out, the challenges of working in an exotic

location, and what good company she was in as an Academy Award nominee.

Playing Against Type

There's an old expression in acting called "playing against type." It seems out of character for an 83-year-old wealthy widow to use swear words, but it's fun to hear my friend cuss once in a while. She looks like a grandmother and can swear like a sailor, on occasion and on purpose, but she knows the difference and when to play with it.

You can work this technique to your advantage, but in a different way. What is your type? Are you, like me, an enthusiastic, blonde cheerleader? Do words spill out of you very easily? For you, less might be more. Still waters run deep. Perhaps you'll seem more intelligent if you don't tell them everything you know, or don't, by talking too much.

If, instead, you are shy or naturally self-conscious, go out of your way to be friendly. Introduce yourself first, offer a genuine compliment, or ask a question that puts others at ease, too.

One man I know is very big and tall. He learned early on to have a good sense of humor. It's how he disarms a situation. By being funny and self-deprecating, he takes away some of the intimidation of his size. Sort of the gentle-giant approach.

Another friend lives her life in a wheelchair. Instinctively, she knows that being surrounded by all that metal creates distance, is sympathy producing, and is not necessarily a conversation starter, particularly with children. But because she's sitting down, she is always at a child's eye level. So, she too, goes out of her way to be funny and outgoing to connect with children. Everyone's favorite little kids can never resist a ride on her perpetual lap!

No Failure to Communicate

The Harvard Business Review reports: "The number one criteria for advancement and promotion for professionals is an ability to communicate effectively."

Obviously, effectively presenting yourself, whether to your peers, your boss, the customer, the general public, or even the media, plays a major role in career advancement.

Is it any wonder that CEOExpress.com, one of the best Websites for executives, includes in its Office Tools section: Citing Sources, Common English Errors, Economist Style Guide, Elements of Style, Guide to Grammar & Writing, Presentation Tips, Press Release Guide, Famous Quotes: Bartlett's Quotations, and QuoteLand.com.

Good grammar is a key to being educated, which is the key to getting ahead. Poor grammar, vulgarity, crudeness, and insensitivity have the opposite effect on your image. It doesn't matter the car you drive, the clothes you wear, or the pen you carry if the words that come out of your mouth are all wrong.

But isn't one person's mistake another's standard or colloquial usage? Sometimes. But if your standard usage causes other people to consider you uneducated, you may want to consider changing it. If you wish to communicate effectively, you should use nonstandard English only when you intend to rather than do it mistakenly because you don't know any better.

Colloquial vs. Common Usage

As a melting pot of peoples and cultures, the fabric of America is rich with colloquialisms. But for a people to communicate, standards have to be set.

Paul Brians, a professor of English at Washington State University, notes that in the debate over Oakland, California's proposed "ebonics" policy, African-American parents were especially outspoken in arguing that to allow students to regard street slang as legitimate in an educational setting was to limit them and worsen their oppressed status. Years of discrimination have taught those parents that the world is full of teachers, employers, and other authorities who may penalize you for your nonstandard use of the English language.

Upwardly mobile parents in the Spanish-speaking and Asian communities of Los Angeles are also eschewing the languages of their homelands in favor of good English. That's understandable and even appreciated in a country created by immigrants who chose American English as their common language. But it's also a little extreme in today's world where being bilingual is a plus and will be expected by others who share your children's heritage. It's best to let your children grow up speaking as many languages properly as possible. Again, the media will help. Television programs and newspapers in native languages as well as English abound and should be encouraged to teach reading, and both proper writing and speaking.

Giving today's student and tomorrow's executive the option of speaking several languages, including Standard English, correctly, is the best gift education can give. But I recently received a thank you note from a new college graduate in which he wrote: "I wish I could of made it to California."

Like many employers, I automatically discard any job applications that contain a common usage or spelling error. My logic is that if applicants could or would make such an error in something as presumably important to them as applying for my job, what mistakes would they make in representing my company to clients? Of course, conversational English is much more casual than written English, but to a well-educated ear, grammatical errors have the same effect as running fingernails over a chalkboard.

When anyone makes grammatical errors, I've always believed that it was how they learned to talk at mother's knee. What loving mother would let her children out of the house speaking in a way that didn't sound good to her ear? So one grows up not hearing grammatical errors as improper or wrong. The good news is that someone with poor grammar usually makes only one or, at most two, basic mistakes over and over again. This makes grammatical errors much easier to correct than you might think because there are usually only one or two key corrections needed!

For me, it's *that* and *which*. If you are defining something by distinguishing it from a larger class of which it is a member, use "that": "I chose the flowers that had the brightest colors." When the general class is not being limited or defined in some way, then "which" is appropriate: "I made a flower arrangement, which impressed everyone."

The secret is hearing what's correct, and using it. Learn your grammatical faux pas. Ask someone who is good with grammar and a good friend, spouse, or trusted coworker who hears your mistakes to correct you. Immediately, if possible, or at least as soon as you are in private. Having a trusted friend, associate, or executive assistant edit your e-mail for grammatical errors is another good way to train your ear to hear what's correct.

How to Say It

Grammar, which knows how to control even kings.

—Moliére

Who knew when we were all falling asleep in 4th grade English that one day Mrs. What's-her-name would prevail? Not knowing how to diagram a sentence bites every one of us in the butt equally when it comes to speaking out loud and communicating by e-mail!

My favorite financial advisor, before I teased him into changing his outgoing voice-mail message, used to say that he would get back to the caller at his "soonest convenience." Nothing really wrong with that, except no one else says it that way! "My earliest convenience" is the accepted phrase and doesn't distract listeners from their intent to leave a message.

Constant reinforcement of good grammar will help you, and so will writing it down, correctly, over and over. Gradually, you will teach your ear to hear and your mouth to speak, correctly.

Here is a brief overview of grammatical do's and dont's. Test yourself to see how much you already know!

Number and Quantity

So many people make this mistake that the distinction may soon be lost from the English language. Things that can be counted should be referred to as fewer (in number), such as birthday candles, cars, and spotted owls. Less refers only to quantity, such as orange juice, pollution, and shoe polish.

Tense

A commonly made mistake is using the past tense instead of the past participle with "have" and "had." This is under-standable because often the past tense of a verb is the same one you use with the past participle. For example, I walk, I walked, I have walked. Far more often, there are three differ-ent words. I ride, I rode, I have ridden. And there are a few more irregulars such as I run, I ran, I have run.

Subjects and Objects

Another challenging grammatical error is subject and ob-ject. To say, "Susan and me went for Chinese" is *incorrect* because you and Susan are the subject of the action or verb. But, "The deliveryman brought Chinese to Susan and me" *is* correct when you are the object of the action or verb.

Agreement

This one is simple: If your subject is plural, your verb should be also.

Making the subject "they" or the object "them" is increasingly done to avoid the dilemma of him/her, he/she. And the sensitivity to gender is a good thing, but not at the price of good grammar. The rest of the sentence should be made plural, too. For example, "They were having the time of their life" should be changed to, "They were having the time of their lives!"

Other ways to get around the gender challenge are to simply eliminate gender-specific pronouns. "An employee who makes (his/her) boss's job easier is the one who will be most valued." Or "An intern needs to have (his/her own) self-direction."

When addressing people of opposite sexes, you will be safe if you treat both equally in a phrase: "ladies and gentlemen," "men and women," "guys and gals," "boys and girls." In business, it's men and women, Mr., Ms., or Dr. It probably goes without writing, but in business, women should never be referred to as: "doll face," "female," "babe," "sweetie," "honey," "my girl," or "the girls in the office."

Modifiers

If you are having trouble with grammar, you are not alone. It's hard to hear good grammar when advertising and TV make grammatical errors. Recently, a computer company had a very powerful billboard campaign featuring the famous faces of Albert Einstein, Mahatma Gandhi, Pablo Picasso, Martin Luther King, John Lennon, Ted Turner, Martha Graham, Jim Henson, Thomas Edison, Alfred Hitchcock, Richard Branson, Muhammad Ali, Maria Callas, Frank Lloyd Wright, and Amelia Earheart. The line was "Think Different." It begged the question, shouldn't it have been "Think Differently," to explain how they thought? Was different meant to be an adverb or an adjective? Did it tell how these people thought or was it a directive or description of "what kind of" thoughts had made them famous, as the advertising agency later contended.

In a sentence, adverbs are often words ending in "ly" and always describe verbs or the action. They answer the questions When? Where? and How? For example, "She played fairly" explains *how* she played. *Not*, "She played fair." It's proper to say, "It's good English," but one speaks English well.

In the phrase, "I have been well cared for," "well" describes the care and answers the question of how I've been treated. In the phrase, "He has taken good care of me," "good" describes what kind of care has been given.

Adjectives describe nouns or subjects by answering which, what kind of, and how many. For example, "It was fair play" (what kind of play).

Foreign Accents

If your native tongue is a European language, the biggest problem you'll have is where to put the accent or emphasis. When an actor wants to give herself a French accent, she stresses the syllable other than the first one because American English almost always accents the first syllable of any word. The romance languages stress a later syllable or the last. It's surprising how much the accent or emphasis on different syllables affects the sound of a word in making you understood. It seems a shame to know the correct word in English and then not be able to communicate using it.

To wit, I once had a delightful French chef with a heavy accent as a client. Our assignment was to reduce the accent and show him how to cook on television. Unfortunately, I could not understand him either. Something about a "lobe stair." Props helped; and when he finally pulled a bright red crustacean out of his pot, I knew he was going to prepare lob stir Bisque!

Americans speak with wide-open mouths, like the country we live in. Asian languages seem to be sung at the back of the throat, so getting your mouth around American words is difficult, too. And yet, speaking English well requires articulation—for everybody.

Articulation

If anyone has ever asked you to mumble that again, or is constantly asking you to repeat yourself, you may have a problem with articulation. For native-born Americans, this is usually simply lazy speech that sounds like there are a bunch of marbles in your mouth. Sometimes it begins as a teenager's shyness and a seeming preference to fall through the floor than to make direct eye contact and speak up, clearly and correctly. But whatever it's origins, there's a sure-fire, easy approach to fixing it!

Mak sur to slo dwn nd mfasize evre sil-able nd sownd, partic-u-lar-ly the ltrs at the ends ov the words. At first, this will probably sound very artificial and stilted to you, but persevere. To others, it will just make you understandable and great to listen to.

A guerilla way of approaching anything you want to change is first to try to do more of the thing you do wrong. Mumble more. Slur your words. Attempt to use poor grammar, on purpose. But not at the office. Notice what you, your mind, or your mouth has to do to get there.

This approach helps to make you more conscious of the bad habit and how you do it. Once you know how you do it, and perhaps why (attention, laziness, habit), you'll have a better idea of how to change it for the better.

Lights, Camera, Action!

Not only will you make thousands of dollars more if your grammar is up to snuff, but you may lose your job if you can't speak correctly. Recently, a brilliant turnaround president was hired, and then fired, by a high-profile company because he spoke in "dems" and "dose" instead of "them" and "those."

He was a street warrior and let loose with expletives, too, that were very inappropriate for the executive suite. Swear words are a fun way to shock your mother as a kid, but in the executive world, it is seen as uncouth and uneducated. So, delete those expletives. Sailors who swear a blue streak need not apply!

Order

And in every sentence, as in life, always put others first. "He and I received our awards." "They gave the awards to him and me." The proper name is correct as either the subject or object of the sentence. "Stacey and I received our awards." "They gave the awards to Stacey and me."

Grammar Practice

Correct the following sentences, even if you can't say what the problem is. The proper English follows.

1. Him and me went over there.
2. Drive safe.
3. It don't make any difference.
4. Yesterday, I done something else.
5. Myself and my friend went.
6. They have wrote about it.
7. Here is the catalog copy which I wrote.
8. They spoke to he and I.
9. I did good.
10. They have believed that all their life.
11. Less people go to that event now that there is less music.
12. I would of done it if they'd only given me a chance.
13. My friend called me off the beach.

Here is the correct grammar to begin to train your ear.

1. He and I went over there. (subject)
2. Drive safely. (adverb)
3. It doesn't make any difference. (agreement)
4. Yesterday, I did something else. (tense)
5. My friend and I went. (subject)
6. They have written about it. (tense)
7. Here is the catalog copy that I wrote. (comparison)
8. They spoke to him and me. (objects of the action)
9. I did well. (adverb describing the action verb)
10. They have believed that all of their lives. (plural)
11. Fewer people go to that event now that there is less music. (number)
12. I would have done it if they'd only given me a chance. (verb)
13. My friend called me from the beach. (preposition)

Some people figure that they will sound stilted or stiff in using proper English, but the truth is that good English is seldom noticed. Poor English always is.

A *Los Angeles Times* reporter stated that it actually made her cringe to quote a celebrity with bad grammar. And a Realtor who represents very expensive beach-front properties, told me a young, wealthy, dynamic entrepreneur gave himself away by using poor grammar. Yet he got angry when she corrected him later in private.

But as the famous line made popular in *Ghostbusters* goes: "Who you gonna call?" If you have an issue with grammar, your friends and coworkers already know it. As you begin to train your ear to question yourself out loud if something doesn't sound right, it's not a sign of weakness, but of courage.

Do you remember Miss Goody-two-shoes who always sat behind you with the right answer? She has probably grown up to be somebody's executive secretary, hopefully with a little more diplomacy. Let her answer your questions. It's in her nature.

The problem is that everybody who prides themselves on grammar has one or more mistakes that irritate them. That's why, if you want to get ahead, you have to speak well all the time—know the right words and use them.

Perhaps the best way any one of us can develop an ear for good grammar is to read. Fortunately, every newspaper and novel in America speaks perfect English! So, read everything that interests you, online and in print: the morning newspapers, business and news magazines, the trades of your favorite sport or hobby. And listen as you read!

Can You Hear Me Now?

Life is a foreign language; all men mispronounce it.
—Christopher Morley, author and journalist

When you take a beach house for the summer, is it primarily to hear the crashing waves, watch the dolphins play in skyblue water, or feel the warm sand between your toes? Your motivation may be the clue to your primary "language" in interpreting the world. In short, your neuro linguistic programming (NLP).

Another way to tell whether people are audio, video, or kinesthetic is to notice how they learn. Copious note-takers are usually videos. If you want to convey something to an audio learner, offer an audiotape package or a book on tape. Kinesthetics learn most from experience, by being there.

Commanding the Orchestra

Because people hear in three different languages, but only one to a customer, it's best to include visual, audio, and kinesthetic words and approaches in your communication. For the audios, you're already on the right track by talking. But do your words have the inflection of a delightful conversation, biting sarcasm, or a dry sense of humor? Do you repeat words or phrases for emphasis? Are you genuinely lively, intriguing, or compelling? Do you use audio words such as "listen," "hear this," "and let me tell you"? If you're droning on in a monotone or with more *uh*'s and *um*'s than words, you'll lose the audios first because they hear *everything*.

For the videos, use visual words such as "see it this way," "my view is," or "looking at it from a different perspective." Word pictures will also go a long way in convincing video listeners. Paint the scene for them, precisely but concisely. Tell it to them in a way that they can see it happening. Give them an unforgettable analogy that shows what you are saying.

National Semiconductor's CEO, Brian Halla, did just that in a keynote address at the 2002 Las Vegas trade show, COMDEX. Mr. Halla compared and contrasted the boom and bust of the Internet, our wired world of fiber optic cable, to the railroad track that was laid end-to-end across the country in the late 19th century. The track was there, the groundwork laid, "But you couldn't give a boxcar away" until another wave of innovation ushered in the refrigerator car, creating a whole new meatpacking industry. Mr. Halla's analogy of boxcars for computer boxes made the point with an audience that will, no doubt, have a hand in the next wave of innovation.

The feeling folks among us need to sense something: laughter, warmth, passion, and excitement. Identify a take-home emotion and then use words and pictures to go with it. In Mr. Halla's case, it was a sense of adventure, pioneering, envisioning a future where no one has gone before.

How do you feel about your topic? What emotion do you want to leave with your audience? Does this situation make you laugh or want to cry? What caused you to raise your voice? How do you show that you are genuinely glad to be here? Is this subject important to you? How will the audience know?

Finally, what do you want from your audience? Sometimes you have to cue them. The late Jack Benny cued his audience that it was time to laugh with folded hands and a pursed-lip pause. On *The Tonight Show*, Johnny Carson was famous for his stay-tuned-for-a-haymaker sideways glance at the camera, straight into every home and funny bone in America.

Actors are teased for asking, "What is my motivation?" Speakers need one, too. One, not many, so the communication is clear. Because it's a safe bet that your audience will include audios, videos, and kinesthetics, your speech or presentation must have something for everyone.

Are you getting the idea that you are the conductor with a whole orchestra at your command? So, now add Commanding to your C-words.

One-on-One Conversation

Speaking one-on-one gives you the advantage of testing your listener for his or her NLP. It's advantageous to know and use each individual's language to enhance communication. For example, if you know someone primarily speaks French, you might begin with "Bonjour."

Certainly, the important relationships of your life should be typecast so you can reach them with the words they can best hear. If they are important relationships, you probably have developed a conversational connection already, but it's helpful to identify each and use the language in your communication with them.

I once had an office of four: I was the video, my salesperson was an audio, and both my business advisor and executive assistant were kinesthetic. Our language probably revealed this daily, but as a visual I learned more by watching. Our offices were in a beautiful high-rise building with high-tech black glass furnishings, art, and breathtaking, panoramic views that reflected my visual taste. The salesperson kept her door closed the entire time so as not to be distracted by other conversations in the office and spent hour upon hour making sales calls and managing client relations by talking on the phone. The managers were very sympathetic to the pressure and climbed the walls when tension was high. By knowing and appreciating each of their languages, and they mine, we could better understand and communicate with each other.

To test the important people in your life, begin by listening to the words they use while observing their habits and values. Audios hear the world. They will use sound words and phrases, play music on their computers, and/or be easily distracted by sound. These hearing folks may be unusually annoyed by a dripping faucet, talk a lot, be into music, and enjoy the sound of the waves more than the sunshine or the vastness of the ocean when they go to the beach.

Kinesthetics feel the world. Their beach experience might be more about the feel of the hot sand on their bare feet or of the ocean breeze. Ask them about their childhood, and you might get a memory of the sweet smells of Gram's fresh-baked apple pie or the luxury of bubble baths.

Videos see the world. They watch the waves crash or the sunset go from crimson to gold. They are always looking into things and will buy a house for the view. We read memories off the television screens of our minds like still-life paintings—take one look and see it all.

And in every conversation, you will get audio and perhaps video cues to identify a stranger's primary language. Eye movements are a giveaway, too. Notice (a visual cue) whether his eyes look up, to the side, or down when he is thinking. Up indicates visual, the side is auditory, and down, toward feelings, is kinesthetic.

Once you have read the people around you, and yourself, you will have a better understanding of how to communicate through language. Being able to use another's approach to the world with appropriate phrases such as "Let's look at it this way," "It sounds to me like," or "My feeling is," reinforces that you are one with them.

If you are unsure, test to see or hear or feel which of the following phrases another is most responsive to: "Do you see what I mean," "Listen to this," "How do you feel about it?" When you hit the right chord, there will be a visible difference in the response. It is like a door opening to you, and you are welcome to walk through it.

Practice listening and looking for others' audio and behavioral cues, too. If you are kinesthetic, you may just sense what the other person needs. Did she buy her car for the color, the purr of the engine, or the smell of new leather?

An equally important aspect of neuro linguistic programming is "mirroring." It is a subtle reflection of another's body language during conversation. Subtly, copy the way he is sitting, what she's doing with her hands, and so forth. Keep reflecting his or her motion or posture until when you change positions, he or she begins to mirror you. That tells you that you are in tune and you can begin to "lead" the dance and ask for what you want.

The host of a very popular and long-running talk show, *Hour Magazine*, was reputed to mirror his guests to put them at ease and enhance their abilities as talk show guests.

Read Your Audience, One Customer at a Time

Is your new client so much a video that too much talking will bore her? Will she take one look at your messy desk or the spot on your tie and doubt your attention to detail? If you are an audio, stop talking and listen to what she says.

If your client is an audio, perhaps you won't be able to get her off the phone. Her e-mails and voice messages may go on and on. Remember that all she knows of the world is what she hears, so if you are a video, try to focus on what she tells you.

Are your client's feelings easily hurt? Is he moody and mercurial? Does he sense when you are happy or stressed? Does he dress for comfort or style? Try to avoid pressuring him to make a decision.

In order to make a good impression, first read people by each one's language and eye movements, then subtly mirror them in conversation and body language. You will hear, see, or feel a connection.

Don't Talk to Strangers

Some enchanted evening...
You may see a stranger
Across a crowded room...

    —*South Pacific*, "Some Enchanted Evening"

Don't let the audience in your crowded room be strangers. Find out all you can ahead of time and keep reading the room until you say, "Thank you." It is both your right and responsibility to know the many aspects of your audience.

Know Your Audience

Because the audience, numbering one to a thousand, is the most important part of a conversation, learn everything you can about the demographics or makeup of the audience ahead of time from whomever arranged the meeting. What city will you be in? What age or age range is your audience? Do they have families of their own? What are their interests? Did they have to pay for this out of their own or their comapnies' pockets? What is the ratio of: sexes, religions, politics, professions, management, staff, etc.?

To paraphrase the five Ws and the H of journalism: Who are they? What do they care about? Where do they come from? When did they decide to attend? Why did they come? And how do you want them to feel about you, your issue, your honoree, etc.?

What are they ready to hear? What insight can you give them? What values, experiences, or goals do you have in common? NOT in common? What do you want them to do as a result of what you've said?

If you don't know who is in your audience and can't find out ahead of time because you don't want to bother a grieving family, have just arrived in the city, or were asked at the last minute, then make a calculated guess. Who would come to this event? Why? Was it required or optional? What unique perspective do you bring? What does this audience want and need from you?

Sometimes, you guess wrong. Once, an audience of fellow alums that I spoke to at Purdue University didn't really want or need what I offered them.

When asked to be the MCs and just "be funny," my co-hostess and I decided to create a mock Academy Awards show and host it as the movie characters Thelma and Louise. Since the movie's screenwriter, Callie Khouri, was also a Purdue alum who had won an Academy Award for her film, her first screenwriting effort, we were at the right place but the wrong time. The average age of the audience turned out to be 73!

Despite the fact that we opened with a film clip of the movie, the audience just didn't know or care who Thelma and Louise were! It may sound cold or selfish, but audiences always listen to the radio station WII-FM (What's In It For Me?).

How can they justify spending the time? What gift do they need from you? How will their experience of this event be better, different, more interesting, entertaining, or enlightening with, than without, you and your words?

Know the Circumstance

Knowing your audience is more than just demographics. It's knowing as much as you can about its circumstances, too. Is the company expanding, or is everyone in fear for their positions? What's happened to the stock price in the last day, week, or year?

Know the Mood

From circumstances, you can take the next and perhaps most important step, be prepared to gauge the audience's mood. Are people bantering when they come in? How do they sit in the chairs—waiting or talking among themselves? Are they comfortable in each other's company? How's business? Are opportunities expanding or contracting? Is it a mixed crowd: managers and staff, doctors and lawyers? This is the most challenging because you can't know the mood until you get there. Read that by the way they engage one another or fail to. Are they smiling at each other and at you OR are peoples' eyes cast downward looking at their shoes, or the ceiling? Are their legs and arms crossed, defensively? Somehow, you must get around that.

This is where knowing good technique and having an adaptive sense of humor comes into play. As the presenter, the leader if you will, you must adapt.

Conversely, is it a fluid or adaptable audience? If audience members are the least bit interested, they will help to shape the presentation to their liking, which will give the presentation more effect.

Know What Time It Is

In a hit titled "Does Anybody Really Know What Time It Is?" the group Chicago went on to ask, "Does anybody really care, about time?"

You should, when it comes to addressing an audience. If it's 8 a.m. on Monday or 3 p.m. on Friday afternoon, you have different challenges. It is said that 10 a.m. Tuesday morning is the business person's best moment of the week, so seize the day and schedule something important, such as your presentation, if possible!

Know the Space

Is it a flat floor with a low or high podium? Is there a stage? How easily accessible is it to the audience?

Now a Republican senator from North Carolina, Elizabeth Dole very effectively broke precedent when she nominated her husband, Bob Dole, for president at the 1996 Republican National Convention. To most everyone's surprise, she left the podium, walked into the audience, and roamed the aisles, with the words, "Now, you know tradition is that speakers at the Republican National Convention remain at this very imposing podium. But tonight I'd like to break with tradition for two reasons—one, I'm going to be speaking to friends. Secondly, I'm going to be speaking about the man I love. And it's just a lot more comfortable for me to be down here with you."

No one fell asleep on Liddy Dole that night, everyone was glued. But what happens if someone is falling asleep, whispering to his neighbor, or not paying attention? The set-up of the room becomes very important at that time. Stand in front of the offender and continue talking. Every time someone begins to nod off or whisper, stand right in front of him and keep speaking.

Use Your Audience

The audience is the other half of your conversation. It's best to involve audience members through acknowledgement, laughter, and poignancy; by name or participation. Learning how to use an audience is the single biggest key to success in a workshop or presentation. Here are some do's and don'ts.

Do's

- Do be your audience's champion. Help 'em win.
- Do ensure that the audience recognizes the value you are offering by applying your expertise directly to current circumstances.
- Do whatever you have to do to engage an audience, on an individual basis.
- Do enable a successful response.

Don'ts

- Don't single out any audience member for critique or ridicule because the group will close ranks against you.
- Don't embarrass anyone, if at all possible.
- Don't take on or criticize the audience as a whole. The audience may close ranks on you and you'll be a dead man walking.
- Don't try to enlist a member of the audience in doing your dirty work. Don't say, "Nudge your neighbor and wake him up for me."

What do you know about your audience? Why are these people important to you as the speaker and why are you and the subject important to them?

In short, what does the audience want or need to know? You will be most successful if you know your audience. Bottom line: The secret to being interesting to audiences is being interested in them.

May I Ask Who Is Speaking?

What's in a name?
—William Shakespeare

One of the most thrilling celebrity experiences I ever had was in meeting Gregory Peck. It was a self-introduction when we found ourselves sort of face-to-face at some function. What impressed me the most was that he stuck out his hand and said, "I'm Greg Peck." Everyone in the whole room, of course, knew the legendary Gregory Peck, even, at the time, 25-year-olds such as myself. But the humility and friendliness of his gesture was unforgettable.

A Million Dollar Secret

With this question, Shakespeare raised a debate for all the ages. And because the number-one rule of etiquette is to make others feel comfortable, saying your name when someone else has forgotten it is very polite, both professionally and personally. It almost always prompts others to say their own names too, and prevents embarrassment especially when someone is trying to introduce people whose names have escaped him.

Saying your first and last name is the sign of an executive. Simply going by your first name denotes an assistant. This used to be mostly true of women secretaries and assistants, but as more men take these positions, they are falling into this habit, too. If you strive to get beyond an assistant position in your career, begin using both your first and last name to introduce yourself on the phone, in person, and in e-mail.

Conversely, if you are looking to take away some of the barriers or intimidation of your position, you may simply refer to yourself by your first name. It tends to level the playing field for others and keeps you closer to the action.

Speaking of names, a million dollar secret I happened to come across early in my marketing career is the practice of asking whomever answers the phone in my most smiling voice, "Hi, who's this?" Without thinking, the person on the other end almost always responds, and suddenly I'm on a first-name basis with the executive secretary, the cold call, the office mate, or the receptionist. I make sure to use his or her name in the next minutes of my conversation and spell it correctly on my contact file, so I can always greet him or her by name when he or she answers the phone again. On the rare occasion that I am met with a sour attitude ("Well, whom were you calling?"), I always explain that I just like to know to whom I'm speaking, and then we're off and running. People like the sound of their own names and the people who take time to know them.

A Rose by Any Other Name

Experts disagree on how best to address yourself, but they all consider it important. Does a formal or old-fashioned sounding name indicate professionalism or make one sound too old or too boring? Does your name make you sound friendly and approachable, seductive, or childish? Be objective.

Unless you are an attorney, middle initials are usually left behind in favor of a first and last name. A hyphenated married name can be a bit laborious too, especially when it is translated to e-mail.

Not enough of us pay attention to the image our names conjure up. Usually, nicknames from childhood are not appropriate on resumes or in the corporate suite. Use your most formal name, Elizabeth. Wait until you are safely ensconced in an office place that finds you indispensable before you casually mention that friends call you Bunny.

Ask yourself what signals the names Destiny, Taisha, Johnny, or Scarlett send. Increasingly, companies are using both first and last names on e-mail so you are further labeled with expectations. In *Romeo and Juliet*, Shakespeare went on to say, "That which we call a rose, by any other name would smell as sweet." But if don't like your name or suspect that it will get in your way, then go by a version of the name that will help you get where you want to go.

When the children of this decade grow up, it may be more common to hire Sages, Destinys, and Kenesaw Mountains, but the time isn't yet.

Experts note that a resume is not a legal document like a job application, but is rather a marketing tool. So let the name you choose for it represent the casual and memorable employee you will be.

This is probably not the first nor will it be the last time that your Stacey, Tracy, Chris, or Pat will have people confused about your sex. Be gracious over the confusion and remember that being a good sport may work to your advantage.

Names will often reveal nationality or heritage. Sometimes, it's a good idea to shorten a foreign-sounding name to initials, or even to add a nickname in quotes. However, one's name IS, after, all, one's name. If you are proud of your name and heritage, by all means use it. Perhaps that way you'll find your place in equality oriented companies with people who embrace diversity.

I know someone whose first name is Gaye, which her mother chose for happiness and light in the 1950s. She now uses her middle name instead because she is heterosexual and doesn't want her name to distract her clients from the business at hand. A firm, once known as Public Relations Aids changed its name too, because everyone confused this brochure and press release–writing company as part of the disease effort.

How could anyone have known, more than two decades ago, what you would grow up wanting to be or how the meaning of a name would change? Most of us do this naturally. We adopt a married name, or don't. We add an *e*, shorten or lengthen our first names, and simply try to get comfortable with our own names as grownups, which is how we identify ourselves to the world.

Let your friends call you by your mother-chosen or childhood nickname, but choose a professional, easy to spell name for yourself, similar in sounds or letters to the one your mother gave you, but more well suited for establishing your career.

One African-American mother named her daughter with both African- and American-sounding names so two decades from now, Olivia Taisha could choose which name better represented her in her world. Will she be a braided rock star who goes only by Taisha, or will she be a corporate lawyer, known as Olivia T. Jones? Only time and Olivia Taisha will tell.

Conversational Credibility

In addition to using your name, an aside, such as, "When I taught at Julliard...," or "At Harvard Business School, I...," or "Writing for the *New York Times* we...," very subtly gives your background and establishes your credibility. So take the time to reduce your curriculum vitae to an appropriate phrase, preferably with an endorser in it. Pick something that is unique to you. For example, a Cajun chef might establish his expertise with, "Growing up in Louisiana...." Most of us didn't do that, so we might enjoy the different flavor of his cuisine.

If you are young, under 30, addressing clients and superiors as Mr., Ms., Doctor, and Professor shows respect and is usually appreciated. At the appropriate time, they will invite you to call them by their first names, often with the friendly chastisement that Mr. is his father and you should call him Jim or Bob or Mark or whatever. Accept the invitation. Unless a woman executive makes it clear that she prefers the salutation Mrs., it has no place in the corporate suite.

An associate of mine once coached a co-founder and chief fund-raiser for a charity. Apparently, she was a highly intelligent woman, poised and articulate...a charming conversationalist. As they began working together to prepare an important fund-raising speech, my colleague asked her some questions: "What has been your experience speaking in front of groups? What do you like about it? What do you not like about it? What happens to you *physically* when you do it?" Her answers were forthcoming and honest. The more she spoke, the more he listened. The more he listened, the more she trusted. One thing she said particularly caught his attention. She was uncomfortable with her name—or, more precisely, with *saying,* her name. "My name is _____." Those words, she confessed, froze her. Her throat would tighten, her voice would shake, her breathing would become shallow—all familiar symptoms of public speaking anxiety.

My colleague is a speech coach, not a psychiatrist, so he didn't delve into the why's and wherefore's, but it was obvious that if your opening sentence always makes you freeze, you will have a hard time warming up. So they talked about her name—where it came from, what it meant, what it felt like when she said it, or when other people said it. They practiced saying it out loud. She said, "My name is..." so many times that she eventually started laughing. The mere repetition had defused her anxiety somehow. Made it funny, less important, less fraught with anxiety. She went home and practiced saying it in front of a mirror. The practice helped. The tightness in the throat transformed into a smile. Warmth and humor crept into her voice and her breathing relaxed. A subtle but profound change was taking place. She was feeling good.

They met again, after her speech. He asked her how it went. "Great!" she said. "I got through the name part easily and after that everything just went fine. People told me afterwards how funny I was."

"Did you raise a lot of money?" I asked.

"Only about $10,000 that night," she said. "But the next day, over $200,000 came in." What's in a name, indeed.

Question and Answer

It's easy if you know the answers.

—Joseph A. Cooper, businessman

My father used to remind his children of this simple truth every time we took exams. Of course, he was right.

"But," clients moan, "what if they ask me something I don't know?" The simple answer is to bridge to something you do know.

My colleague Allen Weiner of Communication Development Associates, Inc., helps allay executives' fears too. "It is just like high school," he explains. "There are four types of questions: A direct question demanding information is like a fill-in-the-blank. A demand for a 'yes' or 'no' is simply a true or false. An open-ended question calls for the blue book essay approach. A multiple-choice question gives you a choice." Nothing could be easier than that, as long as you've studied and are prepared!

The Q&A (question and answer portion) is often the part both reporters and audiences look forward to the most. Your speech or announcement is just a one-way conversation until they get to ask their questions. In press conferences, the press often just waits until the remarks are over before they turn on the cameras or begin taking notes.

According to former San Francisco news anchor Fred LaCosse, journalists fall into a number of types depending on their styles.

The **Machine Gunner** is the type of interviewer who likes to fire off several questions all at once to bewilder and frustrate you. Take control of the interview, and choose one question to answer. Then shut up.

Be careful not to let the **Intruder** confuse you. The Intruder never allows you to finish a thought. You are midway through your message when another question is thrown your way. Take control and finish a thought and then wait for the next question.

The **Paraphraser** is like the game Telephone. When your message is repeated, it often comes out antagonistic and wrong. Make sure you always correct the reporter right then and there.

The **Softsoaper** is a smoothie. He or she is super friendly, but stay alert; remember that nothing is ever off the record.

Hostile is an understatement for the **Bully**. This one is a combination of several types of reporters, plus a few extra nasty habits. Take control, stay calm, and say politely that you are happy to answer the questions if given the opportunity, otherwise offer to reschedule.

The **Sneak** always has tricks up his or her sleeve. Stay on your toes and refer back to your message.

The **Rookie** is an unprepared reporter who requires you to give a lot of background information, which can keep you from getting to the messages you want to convey.

The **Old Horse** is a reporter who is tired of doing the same old stories. Be careful not to mimic him and bore everyone. Establish your own level of energy and keep it up.

Don't let your guard down when dealing with the **Pro**. But appreciate the reality that he or she will give you the opportunity to use your good material.

I recommend thinking of journalists as your boss or your mother-in-law. Nice as he or she is, never forget who they are and where their loyalties lie.

Considered the original "Teflon President" because they said nothing stuck, President Ronald Reagan is a good role model for speakers who are often put on the spot. He pioneered the practice of listening intently to a difficult question. Then he began his answer in the direction of the interrogator, but would finish his answer looking at a more sympathetic member of the press. In essence, he took the floor from the interrogator and avoided getting locked into one-on-one verbal combat.

Bridging the perfect answer is given in a similar manner. It begins with an acknowledgment of the question, then bridges to one of the messages you came to give. We call these SOCOS (Single Overriding Communication Objective Sound bites). They are the three to five bottom-line message points that you want the audience to take home with them. Just choose the one most appropriate to the question and bridge to it.

It is thought that an *and* is always a better bridge than a *but,* which seems to deny or invalidate the whole acknowledgment.

Flagging is a technique that alerts your audience that something important is coming. It is a phrase that sets them up to listen; such as, "I'll never forget the time that..." or "My most embarrassing moment was...."

Another way that the speaker maintains control of the situation is by **addressing** the question *rather than* answering it. Whether the question is a softball, a hardball, or a curve, you can hit it out of the park with a succinct, quotable statement that addresses the question clearly and concisely.

Many politicians make the mistake of giving their SOCOS while seeming to ignore the question. It is much more skillful to use the question to get to your answer. The audience is much more satisfied that you at least addressed the question even if you didn't answer it.

Yogi Berra got around the press once by announcing, before they had a chance to even ask why his team lost a particularly difficult game, "If you ask me a question I don't know, I'm not going to answer."

Of course, everyone isn't Yogi Berra, but the press are people too, and being able to keep your candor, compassion, and humor in any situation garners the respect and admiration of the press and audiences alike.

When there are no questions, one executive usually gets a laugh with, "I've either been exceptionally clear or very confusing."

The practice of repeating a question from the podium is usually very much appreciated by an audience who may not have been able to hear it. Repeating the questions also buys you time as a speaker to think of an answer and allows you to very subtly paraphrase the question to make it more concise and easier to answer. But do it subtly to keep the audience on your side.

I remember once when Ann Landers guested on Regis Philbin's *AM Los Angeles*, she asked every caller to repeat the question. As the associate producer, I asked her during a commercial break if moving the speaker closer would help her hear the questions better. She smiled and said, "Honey, I can hear perfectly well. I just need a little time to consider my answer and the caller needs time to clarify her question."

In both answering audience and media questions, beware of repeating or using *negative* or *loaded* words. Don't let the questioner put words in your mouth, even in denial. Remember that it was President Nixon who was the first to mention the "c" word, "crook." "I am not a crook," headlined every newspaper in the country. Choose your own positive expression of innocence, honesty, and sincerity.

What Should I Wear?

All offices have a uniform. It is usually dictated by the industry, geography, and the boss. The most formal are banks, accounting firms, and law firms. Technology is much more dressed down, and creativity in dress is often required in the arts and entertainment.

The media has kept a refreshing air of formality, perhaps because the networks are based in New York City. When you are a guest, and, perhaps most especially, if you are a brilliant college dropout with a mega-million-dollar software company in Silicon Valley, California, wear the coat and tie. Shirts should be bought to go with the suit and the belt and socks should match the shoes.

The difference between bosses and their heir apparents should only be in the expense of the fabrics, which reflect higher salaries.

Wearing Well

The question is more what *not* to wear. At a recent public relations business breakfast I went to, a young woman showed up in Capri pants and a sheer top. Her name tag announced her as simply, Jennifer. It was no surprise when we learned she had come to sell insurance.

At one Chamber of Commerce event at a ranch in Malibu, I decided to eschew my corporate duds in favor of a cowboy hat, boots, a silk shirt, and jeans. One man came up to me and said, we have a bet that you're in real estate, selling the really expensive houses. Never is it more apparent that you don't get a second chance to make a first impression than with your choice of wardrobe.

Color Me Appropriate

In the art of winning friends and influencing people, it is suggested, at first, to make no impression at all. That's because people are most comfortable with people they perceive to be like them. Over time, of course, your uniqueness will enhance the relationship, but you won't be perceived as so different at first as to be an impossible friend. The same is true with business attire. Seek first to follow the rules that will make you appropriate to the occasion or dress code. In time, you will know how to break them.

To stand out from the background in media and personal appearances, or even show up in color photography, a woman should wear color. Clear, bright, solid color. At the next State of the Union address, notice which senators and congresswomen stand out from the crowd on television. You'll see them in suit jackets of solid red, peacock, turquoise or cobalt blue, Kelly green, or purple.

Notice the president's tie. Although solid red or very small-patterned red ties with white shirts and navy suits are very popular in Congress for their obvious theme of red, white, and blue, did you notice President George W. Bush's choice of ties after 9/11 and throughout the war with Iraq? He chose a series of sky-blue ties that seemed to be an antidote for the fear and hatred of war. A red tie would have merely inflamed the situation, although red is thought to be persuasive in other situations.

Before getting dressed for television, squint your eyes at your wardrobe choice. If the small dots or stripes "dance" before your eyes, avoid them for they will strobe on camera and distract from everything you are saying. Large pictures or patterns, as well as prominent plaids or stripes, which will overpower you, should also be avoided.

Because business attire, as compared to business casual, is still very much a uniform, a man's tie is his signature statement. For a woman, it's her jewelry. Is it antique, delicate, and small? Bold and contemporary? Arty? Expensive? Interestingly, these are the two areas where a personal compliment is appropriate in a business situation. Anything else is too personal.

Like it or not, the uniform for both men and women is still the suit or a version of it for women in a jacket and pants, skirt, or dress. Nothing takes the place of a jacket in looking really professional, on camera or from a podium. To soften the look on certain occasions, women may choose a sweater jacket or sweater set to seem softer and more nurturing, perhaps in a human resources role.

President Reagan was fond of wearing brown suits, which many believed was a subtle way of reducing the intimidating power of the office for a would-be folksy president. A navy blue suit is thought to radiate sincerity while gray is the power color. The darker the gray suit, the more power. Black is usually saved for funerals and Las Vegas. The key to giving an impression of environmental consciousness is khaki or breen (brown-green).

Like the Presidents, use color to subtly accomplish your goals. A pale blue or striped dress shirt is friendlier. If you are young or unsure of yourself, wear a crisp, professionally laundered and starched white shirt to add intimidation to your demeanor for a presentation. If you can afford or need custom shirts for fit, opt for subtle initials on the right cuff if you are aiming for the presidential suite.

PART II

Just Say a Few Words

Working a Room

*Conversation...is the art of never appearing a
bore, of knowing how to say everything
interestingly, to entertain no matter what, to be
charming with nothing at all.*

        —Guy de Maupassant, French author

    Politicians call them meet and greets. Organizations may
call them mixers. Singles call them parties. Bottom line, it's you
in a room full of people you don't yet know, perhaps with name
tags, and the expectation that you will emerge with votes, business cards, or phone numbers.

    All too often, we are thrown back to our experiences as
gawky preteens and the days of cotillion where we were expected to be charming to whichever was the opposite sex!
Horrors.

But now with a clearly defined purpose for networking, perhaps a quota, you may actually enjoy the process. On some level, you know that there is gold in them there hills, or potential clients or dates in them there cliques. It's just figuring out how to prospect for them and mine the gold.

My young associate happened on a technique that serves her very well. Being new to the public relations industry, she can't just walk into a professional gathering like a veteran can and expect conversations to stop so old friends can greet her. She doesn't have any friends yet and always seemed to be on the outside looking in.

Instinctively feeling more comfortable being early than late, she has started arriving when the hosts were setting up and became a greeter as people arrived. This way, she can meet people more or less, one-on-one, make introductions, and the cliques form around her.

This is a great approach, too, for the veteran who doesn't know anyone anymore because "only the newbies go to those things!" But when you are supposed to be the rainmaker and there's not a cloud in sight, go early and graciously greet the literal newcomers. If you are as well known in your industry as you think you are, you will be treated respectfully, as a legend in their midst.

Topics of Discussion

According to the French and many other cultures, Americans have a bad habit of mixing business with everything. In the more refined cultures of the world, business is not appropriate social conversation. Think of nonbusiness topics of discussion such as travel or the arts. To be a well-rounded conversationalist, read up on subjects of interest to you or experience them firsthand. Always remember that you get one point for sharing your own topics of conversation and twice as many for your genuine interest in someone else's.

Stephen Clouse, an on-camera communications coach based in Washington, D.C., recommends observing and then emulating the image of coaches at the end of a sporting contest. The losing coach almost always slouches, head bent over, and eyes looking downward. However, the winning coach stands straight with shoulders back and chin up. He visually communicates the role of a winner and it carries over into gestures and even the smile on his face. He is in awe of the brilliance of his players and humbled at his own good fortune—all is right with the world. "Always be the winning coach on camera and in person," Clouse tells his congressional clients. "That's the type of individual people like to vote for. Ronald Reagan didn't become one of our nation's most likeable presidents by accident, he worked at it."

Likeability

In connecting with an audience, the issue is almost never your knowledge but your likeability. In her book, *How To Work a Room* (HarperResource, 2000), Susan RoAne lists what she calls the Top 10 minglers when meeting new people. Her list is also an excellent "likeability primer." Here are her Top 10:

1. Make others feel comfortable.
2. Appear self-confident and at ease.
3. Laugh at yourself.
4. Show interest by maintaining eye contact, asking questions, and listening.
5. Lean into greetings with a firm handshake and a smile.
6. Convey a sense of energy and enthusiasm.
7. Be well rounded, well intentioned, well informed, and well mannered.
8. Prepare interesting conversational vignettes.

9. Make introductions of others with enthusiasm and compliments.
10. Convey respect and genuinely like people.

Although slightly more than half of your audience connection is made visually, according to Clouse, a whopping 38 percent comes from your vocal quality and delivery.

"It is when you open your mouth that your intellect is judged," Clouse continued. "Governor Bill Clinton spent six months of voice coaching neutralizing his Southern drawl to become a more desirable presidential candidate."

A specific tip Clouse offers is to slow down your rate of speech by elongating the vowels (a, e, i, o, u) for warmth and emotional context. Try extending the vowels with almost any phrase and you will hear the difference immediately.

Another good use of vowels is Mr. Clouse's EO exercise to relax the tension in your face and give you a winning smile. Say the letters E and O out loud, alternately, working your facial muscles. "Of the 19 kinds of smiles including curt and pursed-lip smile, the kind that crinkles the corners of your eyes is the hands-down favorite for showing sincerity. In fact, it will generate an added gift, because it triggers a pleasure center in the brain that causes the receiver to smile back."

Closing Ceremonies

Asking for cards is the closing ceremonies when working a room in the United States and often is a great way to close one conversation and move on to the next.

When you have finished a networking conversation, don't just present your card, even though you may have a box of 5,000 back at the office! Instead, ask for the card of anyone you would like to follow up with or even add to your "Christmas card" list, which is usually a more welcome prospect than going onto your mailing list. Then, stay in touch with them by e-mail, phone, or your next promotional or holiday mailing. As we say in sales, the last you've heard from is usually the first one you think of.

Toasts and Roasts

The Human brain starts working the moment you are born and never stops until you stand up to speak in public.

—Sir George Jessel

This English aristocrat and celebrated trial judge knew of where he spoke. And yet, the occasions where something is celebrated just seem to call for a few words.

Traditionally, the toast was good but boring, and the roast was bad but funny. Today, lines are somewhat blurred between a toast and a roast. In general, the more appropriately personal you can make either one, the more memorable it will be.

The body language of both toast and roast is to raise your glass with your right hand straight from the shoulder. This traditional toasting position indicated friendship in the days when swords or daggers were hidden in the right hand or sleeve for potential attack.

The best toasters and roasters are those who know us best. Recently, I went to a birthday party for a 40-year-old divorcee. Her ex-husband brought the house down while the other roasters were very forgettable.

First, he warmed us up when he said he'd been asked to represent all of the ex-husbands (he is the only one), past boyfriends, and one-night stands. Then, he described the true story of them as a young couple in their early 20s, habitually on game shows while struggling to make ends meet. He conjured up images of *I Love Lucy* as he recounted fondly, and in detail, the time Janet hocked three dining room sets to pay the rent!

A roaster on another occasion merely mentioned, in headline fashion, the dramatic moments of the honorees' life leaving the stage for the guest of honor to tell his own great stories.

Depending on your time, talent, and resources, you can get very creative. One roaster I know, who can belt out opera with the best of them, arranged for a piano and piano player at a August retirement party. Her adaptation of "Summertime" from *Porgy and Bess* made everyone in the audience a little envious of the honoree's imminent summertime, when the livin' is easy.

Take a point of view (coworker, next-door neighbor, best friend in college, bride and groom's matchmaker, grew up together), and find something of value in it for the occasion. Trust the person who asked you or yourself for volunteering. There's an old saying in Hollywood, What's my motivation? Ask yourself, *Why am I doing this?* To get attention for myself or focus attention on the guest of honor? It always helps to know the motivation you have for speaking. What do you want to accomplish? Why are you interested in talking with this audience? What does it hold for you? What do you have for it? What funny, endearing things doesn't the audience know about the honoree...yet?

What will be added if you speak in this situation? What would be lost if you don't speak? Being clear about your motivation and what you can offer helps to give purpose, which helps to conquer fear.

Weddings

A wedding is often the first opportunity most of us have to toast, or gently roast, our friends. An essential ingredient of any wedding, toasts have several functions, not the least of which is to bridge from the formal to informal. After a few toasters express the happy feelings of everyone, both the bride and the groom, and their friends and relatives can begin to relax and enjoy themselves.

The best man always begins the series of toasts by addressing the bride or bride and groom, and the father of the bride concludes them by welcoming everyone and commanding that the festivities begin.

With families being newly introduced to each other and the usual mix of generations, it's important to be humorous but appropriate. According to a recent survey in *Modern Bride*, nearly one in five brides were mortified by the best man's toast! A good rule of thumb is, when in doubt, leave it out.

The old standby of "unaccustomed as I am to this" is probably not going to win listeners over to your side either. It's also much too self-conscious. A wedding I recently went to featured a very young best man who pleaded with the audience for understanding, as it was the first toast of his career. The entire reception was pulling for him to pull it off, but his pulling it off was all that I remember—*not* whatever he said about the bride and the groom. It's their day; you should feature them instead of your own insecurity.

Again, ask yourself, *What uniqueness can I add? Why am I here?*

"Because I have to be" is not a good answer, although, it may be the first thing that comes to mind. The father of one groom, who was uncomfortable with the people who would be his son's new in-laws asked my screenwriting partner for help in crafting his rehearsal dinner toast. The KISS principle was never more necessary. "Keep It Short, Sweetheart."

Together, they explored that he really only wanted and needed to do three things: proclaim pride in his son, acceptance of his new daughter, and happiness in meeting her family.

This is what he said: "My son always strives for the very best. Whether through dumb luck or sheer determination, he has made no exception to that rule in taking a bride. He's always made me very proud, but never more happy that in choosing a wife of such fineness and grace. I am pleased to be joining with her family in celebrating these remarkable young people and the remarkable life they will have together."

My own dear father's simple and sincere toast at my wedding, which I still remember decades later, was, "May you always be as happy together as you are today."

And the wedding toast I traditionally give when it feels like more toasts are needed is a variation of the song "May You Always" with original words and music by Larry Markes and Dick Charles. Being careful not to race through it, I always take time to get the words across.

May you always walk in sunshine
Slumber warm when night winds blow
May you always live with laughter
For your smiles become you so
May you always be dreamers
May your wildest dreams come true
And may you have found someone to love
As much as we love you.

Traditionally, the men give the toasts, but with today's non-traditional families of single mothers, divorced matrons of honor, young grandmothers, and grown children, everyone who knows the couple is welcome. Here are some thoughts and phrases to work into your toasts.

For better or for worse, but never for granted.

—Groom

Today, I have married my best friend.

—Bride

In Genesis, the Bible says that it is not good for man to be alone. So God created you for me.

—Groom

If it weren't for marriage, men would spend our lives thinking we had no faults at all.

—Married best man

May you never forget what is worth remembering and never remember what is best forgotten.

—Mother of the bride

May "for better or worse" be far better than worse.

—Father of the groom

Mythologist Joseph Campbell wrote, "When you make a sacrifice in marriage, you are sacrificing not to each other, but to unity in a relationship."

—Mother of the groom

If you steal, may you steal one another's hearts. If you fight, may you fight for one another.

— Maid of honor

Martin Luther said, "There is no more lovely, friendly and charming relationship, communion or good company than a good marriage."

—Matron of honor

In *The Prophet*, Kahlil Gibran writes: "Think not that you can guide the course of love, for love, if it finds you worthy, guides your course."

—Grown daughter

Now will you drink with me...that your love guides you through life and echoes in eternity.

—Father of the bride

The entire sum of existence is the magic of being needed by just one other person.

—A single best man

Socrates said, "My advice to you is get married: if you find a good wife you'll be happy; if not, you'll become a philosopher."

—A divorced best man

Poet and playwright, Oscar Wilde, said, "Woman begins by resisting a man's advances and ends by blocking his retreat."

—A divorced best man

Marriages may be made in Heaven, but man is responsible for the maintenance work.

—A married best man

I share Goethe's wisdom with you, "We are shaped and fashioned by what we love."

—Grandmother of the groom

All women should know how to take care of children. Most of them will have a husband someday.

—Grandmother of the bride

A toast should always end with a formal indication to the guests that they should join you in toasting to Adam and Eve's happiness. "To Adam and Eve!"

An interesting addition to the 21st century are online books and services that professionally write for you or help you edit your own wedding toasts. According to the *Wall Street Journal*, there is big business for these services that offer to work magic in 24 hours and mostly under $100. Other online help provides fill-in-the-blank templates to help you get started.

Birthdays and Other Occasions

For birthday toasts, I often borrow simple sentiments from birthday cards. My most recent favorite is, "To one who is much too young to be this old."

And there is no limit to the fun one-liners you will find at your favorite card store without spending a dime. Or instead of giving a $10 bottle of wine, buy up to three cards with great lines, use them in your toast, and give them as your gift. They will seem more personalized and last a lot longer than the wine.

Obviously, a toast can be a speech or simply raising a glass and offering a cultural tribute. In Sweden, it's "skol." Japan, it's "compai," and in Britain, it's "cheers." There is a rumor that to raise a glass of anything nonalcoholic is bad luck. Seems to me that missing a chance to wish someone well is a greater detriment to your karma than toasting with your beverage of choice.

If you are the recipient of a toast, you do not stand, raise your glass, or take a sip of your drink, but you do thank the toasters or at least smile and graciously nod. You are not obliged to propose a toast in return.

Awards and Acceptance Speeches

It takes three weeks to prepare a good ad-lib speech.

Mark Twain

Giving awards has become a popular way to get attendance at events. It was once suggested to me as the program chair for a fund-raising dinner. The challenge was how to get women business owners to spend hard-earned dollars to come to the fund-raising banquet. Someone who had been in public relations for a long time suggested creating the first-annual Celebrity Woman Business Owner Award. We sent letters to several celebrity women who were in business with clothing lines, retail stores, restaurants, and food products. They all said yes, so we had honorees for the next several years. In fact, the national chapter borrowed our local idea and celebrity woman business owner Olivia Newton John for its event, too.

This becomes a win-win for everyone because the high-priced publicists who promote the stars are always looking for new celebrity angles and can't help but mention your organization, along with perhaps the time, date, and price in publicizing their recipient. This is also used effectively among giant corporations and law firms that will usually take a number of tables in literally paying tribute to their honoree!

There are two sides to an acceptance speech: Giving the award and making the acceptance.

A good technique for giving the award is to save the recipient's name as the last thing you say. Even though everyone may know whom you are talking about, it creates some suspense and a payoff.

Whichever role you play, do your research for some little known but charming and relevant facts about the recipient and/or the award. If something interests or pleases you, it is likely to do that for the audience, too.

At a UCLA scholarship awards ceremony I attend every year, the fun is in the novelty and variety of the students' speeches in accepting their scholarship awards. The audience is made up of benefactors who provide the dollars and enjoy learning of the difference the money makes in these underprivileged students' lives.

One young man announced that he was the happiest of all the students to receive the award because, unlike the other recipients who were pursuing medicine and law, he was a philosophy major and would, obviously, have a tough time getting a job!

A young medical student came directly from making rounds in scrubs with a stethoscope around her neck—she gave her appreciation in two languages, as her parents only spoke Spanish.

A young Armenian brought his high school teacher for recognition as his mentor. The grandfatherly teacher shared the podium with his former student, acknowledging that the cost of college back in his day was only $36 a term. "Thanks to your scholarship program, today's deserving students like Josef are getting this fine UCLA education, too."

Families were mentioned who did all they could to put food in their kids' mouths. Without the scholarship, an education would have been totally out of reach. One young man pointed with pride to his mother who had taken a six-hour bus ride to be at the ceremony. Another student acknowledged that he really appreciated the sacrifices his mother had made too, even though she had only bussed in from Pomona, which is a 30-minute commute. The running joke for the event became a competition of whose mother had spent the most hours on a bus to get there!

I once coached a corporate executive to present a check at a celebrity golf tournament. Because there was nothing inherently interesting or novel in the ceremony, we had to dig for something to give it meaning. Turned out that he'd always loved the game of golf, but as a kid with a handicap, he could only watch. Now, he felt like he was finally playing the game.

The biggest mistake to make in accepting an award is making your acceptance speech too long or too political. Your audience may not share your politics. At the twice-canceled Academy Awards that took place in the heat of the United States' war with Iraq, the stars were appropriately chastened about using the forum as an anti-war bully pulpit. But one documentary filmmaker piped up in a call for President Bush's resignation. The immediate reaction was that as the saying goes, he won't have lunch in this town again. And he may not have much work either.

A recent recipient of a homeless shelter award angered the million dollar corporate sponsor by launching an attack on big business in America.

So, stick to the subject and event at hand and mine for the poignancy to give meaning to an otherwise superfluous and tedious exercise for an audience.

Acceptance speeches, with few exceptions, are almost always too long. Lines such as: "It all began..." or "I was born in a simple log cabin in Illinois..." or "My birth as it was later told to me..." and even, "It was a dark and stormy night..." are cultural jokes that poke fun at the idea that there will now be a review of your life as a novel instead of a simple thank you.

If an after-dinner speech is text, the acceptance speech is shorthand. It probably needs to be more than just a heartfelt thank you, but often not a lot more. Look to the awards ceremonies such as the Emmys, Grammys, and Academy Awards. Decide which recipients you like and why, and who you'd like to emulate.

When you are competing for an award, take your lead from sports where every player and team genuinely compliment their opponents. This is a win-win situation, particularly for you, because if you lose, you said yourself that they were really good and if you win, you appear to be that much better.

In particular, when your acceptance speech is the result of winning over others in a competition, don't give a speech but rather a thank you. Again, look to professional athletes who follow the practice of "less is more" when they win. You can be pleased but not proud. Make yourself the example of a lesson learned, but never the hero. That is too much like bragging, which turns everyone off.

If you are accepting an award that is an acknowledgement of your service, part of everyone else's acknowledgement is an acceptance of sitting through what you have to say. Don't take advantage and go on too long.

One story goes that Yogi Berra was receiving the key to New York City on a miserably hot and humid day. Mayor Lindsay's wife, Mary, commented on how cool he looked, and he replied, "You don't look so hot yourself." Later, he reflected, "I guess I was a little nervous about the speech I had to make."

After-Dinner Speeches

A difference of taste in jokes is a great strain on the affections.

—George Eliot
(pseudonym of Marian Evans Cross)

To joke or not to joke becomes the question for an after-dinner speech. Because your mission is to entertain rather than educate, jokes do have a place, but stories with surprise endings are safer. Search for a personal anecdote or colorful metaphor, out of which springs an unexpected, unanticipated perspective. Make it personal so you can laugh at yourself, not others

The downfall for most after-dinner speakers is to tell a joke to get the attention, then spend the next 20 minutes making a point no one cares about. You can have substance without style, but you cannot have style without substance. President Clinton tried to memorialize the close of the 20th century in his second Inaugural Address with flowery phrases that said nothing. It is what I call a "Laundry List" speech. He said:

Along the way, America produced the great middle
Class and security in old age, built unrivaled
Centers of learning and opened public schools
to all, split the atom and explored the heavens,
invented the computer and the microchip, and
deepened the wellsprings of justice by making
a revolution in civil rights for Africa-Americans
and all minorities and extending the Circle
of citizenship, opportunity and dignity to women.

All true, but so what? There was no point. And it never got any better. Don't try to be profound without a point because you end up pontificating about nothing. Thereby wasting everyone's time and this moment in history, which will never come again.

Beginning, Middle, and End

Make your speech a metaphor or personal anecdote. Give it a middle, a surprise, and a laugh. The best after-dinner speech is a three-act play. Act I: Set up, Act II: Unexpected turn of events that produces a conflict, Act III: The climax, then, the resolution of the conflict. Problem solution, stumbling blocks along the way. Both *Bull Durham* and *Field of Dreams* are about going back, unexpressed love, father to son, and missed opportunities. Playing baseball is not the story. Life is the story told as a baseball game.

Start with a personal, real-life story that taught a lesson or personified some truth. Make yourself the butt of the joke, *never* the hero or heroine.

Having one or several core speeches that can be customized to the audience means that you don't have to reinvent the wheel or start from scratch each time. You know a speech better after you have given it, you learn what points, jokes, and stories work with an audience and which don't. Hindsight, after all, is 20/20. But customize your past remarks by reading up on the event, and the company, and satirize the biggest names and most important people they have. I often critique the ties of the men who introduce me. I tell them I'm going to do it, so they dress accordingly.

The Spoken Word

If you do choose to write your speech out as a security blanket, write for the ear, not the eye. Remember that your audience is, hopefully, listening—not reading.

Remember that the spoken word must be simpler and much easier to comprehend than the written word, which can be taken at the reader's own pace and reviewed until understood. The spoken word flies by and is gone, forever. So you must slow down your spoken message and keep it simple, letting it sink in.

Read your words out loud, first for yourself, then to a candid but compassionate friend or friends to see how well you can say them. If your words confuse, you have trouble saying them, or you run out of breath, write them in shorter, more simple sentences. Peggy Noonan, *Good Housekeeping* contributor and speechwriter for former presidents Ronald Reagan and George W. Bush, writes in her book *Simply Speaking*, "where you falter, alter."

Winston Churchill used dashes to break up his sentences and indicate where he should take breaths. My clients are also encouraged to use big type down the center of the page, much like a TelePrompTer. "Underline for emphasis," I tell them, "use a single slash for a short pause, a double slash for a long one, put in a stick figure where you want to gesture, and a smiley face where you want to smile."

Acronyms

Even though every industry has it's own jargon, it's important to spell out acronyms after using them, just to make sure that everyone in the audience is on your page.

This is particularly helpful, even with technical audiences, where the same acronym may have two different meanings and context does not always clarify it. For example, IP can mean both intellectual property and Internet protocol.

Leave Them Laughing

Jokes are very risky unless you are a member of the group you are poking fun at and you have a joke they've never heard or want to hear every time. Comedians such as Shelly Berman and George Carlin, Dane Cook and John Stewart, Billy Crystal and Mort Saul are like watching *Casablanca*: layered, textured, dynamic.

When preparing your message, avoid the temptation to gather more and more facts. You probably already know 100 times more than your audience knows or wants to know on your subject. Spend your time taking an interest in audience members and really exploring what they could gain from you. Narrow the focus of your message so they will go home with one easy-to-remember point supported by three easy-to-follow sub-points. The geniuses I've known have always made things so simple and easy to understand that they made me feel smart too! Not bad for a night's work.

And the Moral Is

It is death to start a speech with, "Tonight, I'm going to talk to you about...." Instead, build rapport from the introduction or circumstance, followed by an attention-getting story and a provocative but appropriate moral, statement, or question as the main point. Now, mention who the audience is on this occasion:

members, contributors, volunteers, and employees, and why this point will be important to them. Now, add your credentials as an expert in bringing this message to them and preview each of three sub-points, detail each, review them all and wrap it up with the point again, stated somewhat more profoundly.

On page 143 is a fill-in-the-blank Presentation Pyramid pioneered by Allen Weiner of Communication Development Associates that I've used in coaching for the last decade. It illustrates that a speaker must grab the audience's attention before they will focus on the point. Then, they must know what's important about it before they care about your credentials in bringing it to them. Stop here if your goal was simply self-introduction. Otherwise, as you will remember from the 8th grade speech class, tell them what you are going to tell them, tell them, and tell them what you just told them. Finally, clarify the point as a take-home message.

The Do's and Don'ts

Probably the most often-asked question of speech coaches is: What should I do with my hands?

One thing not to do is jiggle the change in your pocket. Watch sports coaches on the sidelines of important games: Are they wondering about body language and what to do with their hands? Basically, their hands and faces and bodies are doing whatever it takes to get the point across.

Avoid hanging on to the podium. Stand with your feet about 18 inches apart, depending on your height, and one slightly ahead of the other. Sink into one hip to look more natural.

A well-deserved sense of self-confidence comes from being more conscious of the gift you have to share than in being overly conscious of your self. How do you stand when you sincerely want to convince someone? Chances are you don't rock back and forth to the tune of your own sing-song voice.

There was a television commercial once that memorialized the line "You can't fool Mother Nature." You can't fool all of the audience all of the time, either. Listeners know how you feel about what you say from the sound of your voice.

If your inflection goes up at the end of a sentence, you're questioning yourself. When we make a statement we believe in, our voices drop at the end, leaving no question that we believe in what we are saying. So, say what you believe and believe what you say, and your voice will reflect it.

Really don't know what you have to offer? Hire someone to help you. The yellow pages have speechwriters and so does the Internet. There's no shame in getting some perspective. I've often said, for professional results, go to professionals. Like any good counselor, they can help you talk out your stumbling blocks and coach you.

And there's no shame in saying no to a speaking engagement or keynote that you would rather not do. "Just say no" before anyone is counting on you, because you can be sure that if you don't like the audience, they won't like you.

Being memorable means that someone in the audience was touched by an idea, an inspiration, a memory, a smile. As a speaker, you have a mandate to convince, persuade, inspire, and cajole. Go for it.

You can probably do anything for 20 minutes, including give a speech. As Ms. Noonan reminds us, President Reagan always said that no speech should be longer than that. He used the logic that if a few minutes were long enough for the Gettysburg Address and the Sermon on the Mount, it is long enough for any audience.

The Democrats were not always as succinct. Even President Clinton's early supporters bemoaned how much he seemed to love the sound of his own voice in his speech in which he nominated Michael Dukakis at the 1988 Democratic National Convention. And as one-time presidential hopeful

Hubert Humphrey was reminded by his wife, "Darling, for a speech to be immortal, it need not be interminable."

Presentation Pyramid

Rapport Builder (optional)

Attention-Getter

Main Point

Importance to Audience

Credentials

Preview

Body

Review

Main Point Summary

Arguments and Apologies

19

I have found you an argument; I am not
obliged to find you an understanding.

—Samuel Johnson

In arguments, as in sports and life, whether you win or lose depends a lot on how you play the game. One of the best ways to make your points is to avoid blaming the other and take responsibility for your own feelings.

Instead of, "YOU did such and so," try saying, "What happened made me feel disappointed, hurt, sad, lost, or betrayed because...." I statements, as they are called, keep the responsibility for your feelings with you. Your worthy opponent, instead of feeling blamed and becoming defensive, can usually at least sympathize with your feelings. He or she then has the option of mirroring back what he has heard; expressing understanding, sadness, or regret; and offering to do something to help you feel better if she or he cares to. If not, you still have a clear understanding of how you feel and perhaps how he or she feels about you.

If you are in an argument where blame is being leveled at you, justifiably or not, try this in reverse by stating the feelings that would seem appropriate to the situation. For example, "That must have made you feel disappointed, hurt, sad, lost, or betrayed." If you identify the correct feeling, it's like throwing a life raft to a drowning soul. Suddenly, she is heard, as if by magic, and she will elaborate and expound on the feelings you've correctly identified. Even if you guess wrong, you've taken the argument to a feeling level and your contrarian will almost always come back with the correct feeling. Now you have the chance to acknowledge the feeling and express sadness and regret and offer to do something to help her feel better if you care to.

Sometimes, the best question to ask is, "What can I do to make you feel more cared for, understood, trusted, accomplished, successful, and respected?" By involving your opponent in the solution, you guarantee that you've gone to the heart of the matter and will find out what to do next if you care and can.

This technique of active listening deepens surface conversation, too. By identifying the feelings that come up in any situation, people seem to feel not only heard but understood as well.

Fighting fair means limiting the argument to the issue at hand and not condemning the other person's character or being. Follow the same principle that good parents do with children: *I don't like how you are behaving but I value, honor, respect, and love you.*

Just as in other communications, arguments and avoiding them take planning and know-how. A senior citizen I know avoids getting baited into arguments when her grown children call for advice, money, and other things children call on their parents for. "I don't always agree with how they are running their lives," she says, "but I've schooled myself in letting their problems remain their problems with an, 'of course that's between you and him.' Then, I graciously say goodbye and quickly get off the phone." After some knock-down drag-out fights that upset her more than anyone, she began to keep notes at her desk of what she calls her "noncommittal phrases." "I just listen and then use one of these to get off the phone. It keeps me from having to defend myself or anyone else and getting pulled into their grievances and accusations."

Another good exercise is to offer a simple statement. Paraphrase what you've said without judging or condemning. "What I understood you to say is..." you haven't aligned or opposed, you just said in other words so the other person knows they've been heard not just listened to. The dynamic in most arguments is that neither party is listening. Each is only awaiting his or her turn to argue and is not paying any attention to the other. As soon as I know I've been heard, it either satisfies me or cuts the ground out from under me.

Apology

Confession of our faults is the next thing to innocence.

—Publilius Syrus

In Chapter 7, notice that of all the distinguishing characteristics of different cultures, the one noted for the United States is acknowledging wrongdoing and apologizing. America's Puritan heritage is nowhere more evident than in its reverence for truth. It is locked in there with justice and the American way. Falling on your sword is revered here as in no other country or culture.

The best antidote for regret was shared by the well-known journalist Jim G. Bellows, who is perhaps the most prolific editor in the history of journalism. With assignments that included the *Atlanta Journal, Detroit Free Press, Miami News, New York Herald Tribune, Los Angeles Times, Entertainment Tonight, ABC News,* and *TV Guide,* Jim Bellows follows the guiding principle of "begin at once and do the best you can."

Missteps

It is a humbling experience for the person fortunate enough to get the call from a friend who wishes to make amends as a requirement in the celebrated 12 Steps of Alcoholics Anonymous. There is no dependence on whether you accept or not. The call is simply made to right a wrong or correct a mistake, which southern California holistic therapist Dr. Sue Colin terms a misstep.

In *The One Minute Apology* (William Morrow, 2003), authors Margret McBride and Ken Blanchard recommend realizing and admitting your mistakes as a first step. "Be completely honest with yourself and take responsibility for your mistake before you apologize," they suggest. "At the core of most problems is a truth you don't want to face. Problems spin out of control the minute you avoid dealing with them.

"Apology begins with surrender and ends with integrity. Honesty is telling the truth, integrity is living the truth, consistently."

Once you've acknowledged your wrongdoing, you must correct the wrong and make amends. Be genuinely sincere about earning (winning) back love and trust. It can be a very creative process. Some of my best relationships have begun with a mistake or misstep, because it cracked the shells of our understanding.

In the 1953 production of *Time and Time Again,* James Hilton wrote, "If you forgive people enough you belong to them, and they to you, whether either person likes it or not—squatter's right of the heart."

Make apologies brief and sincere. Recap what you did. How it hurt the other person or situation. Acknowledge how you feel about it.

Accept apologies graciously by briefly mentioning the impact of the other's actions and how you felt, and then offer to move on. If you can't, then at least acknowledge your appreciation for the courage it takes to apologize.

Correct something as soon as you realize it's been misconstrued or misunderstood. Whose responsibility is a misunderstanding? The first person who becomes aware of it.

In the media, one of the most important aspects of apology is timing. It's not only what did you know and when did you know it, but what did you say and when did you say it. Here, too, McBride and Blanchard's caution applies, "The longer you wait, the more the weakness will be seen as wickedness."

Lead from a position that responsibility has not yet been determined, unless it has, then move directly to ways in which your company is reacting in a respectable manner. Don't meet the media and deny it was you if it was. (You should know!)

The minute you know you are wrong, begin at once to do what's right. If your company was in part responsible, show as well as tell that specific actions have now been taken to ensure that the situation will not—cannot—be repeated.

Conversations

When you fall into a man's conversation, the first thing you should consider is, whether he has a greater inclination to hear you, or that you should hear him.

—Sir Richard Steele (*The Spectator*, no. 49)

In conversation, are you just waiting for your turn to talk? Or are you paying undivided attention by listening without interrupting? Do you allow your cell phone to interrupt your conversations, thereby trying to have two conversations at once, both in person and on the phone?

By looking too disinterested in your audience or turning your attention away from the dialogue, you risk offending or losing an audience of any size from one to one thousand. Attention and engagement, more than content, set the tone of a conversation. Paying undivided attention is not about talking, it's about listening without interrupting to talk about yourself.

When you ask a question, make sure it's something you really want to know.

Of President Bill Clinton, it's often been said that "he makes you feel as though you are the only person in the room." He does that with eye contact and a total focus on what you are saying.

Too often, we don't have the courage to "just say no" to a conversation we don't have time for or interest in. So, we are half-listening or just waiting for our turn to talk. That's not fair to others or even ourselves.

In order to be authentic, make sure that every conversation you engage in has some value for you. If it isn't obvious, look for it. Perhaps you are learning something or taking the next step in a process or being a sounding board for another person. Just make sure that you make the choice to spend this time in this way and then commit yourself to it, totally.

Every conversation has a process, which begins with an attention-getter or greeting. In a phone call, it can be a "hello" or simply saying the recipient's name in a voice that's recognizable as you. Then there's the courtship where you establish the relationship that will build the comfort to continue. Here is where you clarify the value for the audience to (1) speak about himself, his ideas, experiences, problems or (2) learn something of value from you. Asking whether this is a convenient time before you launch into your agenda is polite but can be counterproductive by stopping the conversation before you've had an opportunity to show value to the one you've called. Listen carefully to the voice on the other end, though. You'll know soon enough whether you have chosen the wrong time. The rapport-building can range from a "How are you?" to an inquiry into a recent event or it may only be a half sentence to bring the recipient up to speed.

Bridging to the point of the contact happens in the middle quickly or eventually, depending on the context and the time available. Establishing rapport takes intention, a plan, patience, and follow-through to accomplish, but it is building the groundwork for this and future conversations. More of this so-called small talk is required when the speakers are strangers trying to find common ground. But reestablish it as much as necessary every time, even when you know the person well, because situations, moods, and facts may have changed since the last time you spoke.

Role of the Listener

In the art of conversation, the listener is in the power position. It's not just words that command attention.

It's facial expression, body language, gestures, reactions—all the currency of paying attention. The most important thing in any conversation is that each participant knows that she or he is being heard. Listening communicates value to the speaker.

As in the film *My Dinner With Andre*, the listener can do more to direct the conversation than even the speaker. Because, as Roger Ebert points out in the *Chicago Sun-Times* (1999), what the film exploits is the well-known ability of the mind to picture a story as it is being told. As the listener, encourage the speaker with a smile, body language, and intelligent questions. Compliment other people in your conversation to avoid seeming critical or putting anyone on the defensive.

Speaking before an audience of any size is really having simultaneous one-on-one conversations. It's a very efficient way to communicate.

Conversations must be a friendly version of an argument. Otherwise, they are just baby pictures on an airplane. If you are just waiting your turn to speak about your pictures, it is two interspersed monologues. Each participant must be willing not only to share what's familiar to them, but to break new ground.

Take the opportunity to explore things you have never considered or felt before. It's an opportunity to stretch. The response will be a mystery. Within that uncertainty lies possibility... something thought about but not yet discussed. Dreamed about but not yet realized.

A really good conversation can be the first step in realizing something entirely new in your life. Tell your new experiences to others in exciting ways. My jumping off place is that I don't know something, yet.

Conversation provides a way to learn from each other. All too often, parents, bosses, and teachers conduct monologues and lectures rather than assigning value to the perspective of an offspring, employee, or student and benefiting from it.

The biggest block to a conversation and hearing what the other person is saying is *"Yes, but."* Instead, try, *"Yes, and."*

Here are some other rules to enhance the communication of your next conversation:

Rules for Conversation

Do's

- Do be well-read.
- Do be willing to expose your ignorance.
- Do avoid wasting time in conversations where there is no contribution you can or want to make.

Don'ts

- Don't pretend agreement or interest.
- Don't be a spectator to the conversation. Get involved.

The best conversations seem to be ones where we don't debate or strive to impress, but are open to learning and pursuing mutual problem-solving. A problem to solve is better than a complaint over a chronic condition of life.

Job Interviews

It is never too late to be what you might have been.

—George Eliot
(pseudonym of Marian Evans Cross)

Designing or redesigning a career illustrates that most of us are better at positioning products and companies than we are at positioning ourselves. Many of us are so self-critical that we fail to enjoy the journey, but if you think of yourself or your purpose as a project and give it a "handle" or a name, it's easier to grab on to. For example, my company, Ready for Media, has always been much easier to market and sell than Anne Ready Productions would have been because it's created by me but it's not about me.

Whether you are guesting on a talk show or in a job interview, "Sit on your feet and think on your seat." That means to sit up straight with your head up, shoulders back for relaxed but full breathing, comfortably perched on the front half of your chair.

You will feel almost as much energy as if you were standing, pushing against the floor with your feet. Notice that on the network morning shows on the alphabet stations, the hosts assume this position, particularly on sloppy chairs and couches, to appear bright, interested, and involved in the interview. Do the same in your interview. It not only helps you look better, but think better as well.

One seasoned job applicant thought well and quickly in an interview by answering the question, "Did you ever make a mistake?" with "Sure, I'm certainly human. But I never made a mistake that I didn't fix before it became a disaster." A perfect example of candor, creativity, and confidence. He didn't go into dangerous and damning detail about the errors of his ways; instead, he answered the interviewer's "unasked" question of whether they could count on him to help the company survive and succeed, particularly in crisis.

Most interviewers have just such a favorite loaded or negative question or two to separate the wheat from the chaff. One of my favorites is a version of "Now that you've presented your strengths, what do you consider your greatest weakness?" It's another opportunity for you to be concise, candid, and charismatic. Very often, what bugs you the most about yourself and you consider to be a fault—preferring to work alone, being compulsively neat, getting lots of input before making a decision—is just what the employer is looking for in the office mix.

Think of each job interview as another time at bat in the game of your career. It's when you strike out that you learn the most. And as Yogi Berra said 30 years ago when the Mets were about nine games out of first place in the middle of the summer. "It ain't over till it's over." They went on to win the division.

The philosopher Soren Kierkegaard said life can only be understood backwards, but it must be lived forwards. The same is true for careers. No one is ever quite sure where a business career path will lead. We gradually get to know what we're good at, but often neglect what we could be good at.

Most of us grow up with a certain set of blueprints, based on our parents' expectations of what our careers and lives should look like. But they were never us, living in our time. So, when opportunity knocks, things are presented that may not necessarily be in your script. Consider them carefully, anyway.

The "F" Words

While you are learning the skills to *flourish*, don't be ashamed to *fake* it until you make it. This does not mean lying or being deceitful. It means acting "as if" until you really know how. As Yogi Berra said, "You can observe a lot by watching." Notice what successful people do.

Beliefs influence actions. Actions influence habits. Habits influence character. Character influences destiny. So look to your beliefs. Are you flourishing there?

The number-one concern parents usually have is who their kids' friends are—who they hang with. What are they learning? In parenting yourself and guiding your career, what can you learn from the people around you who are the more creative, successful, talented, disciplined, organized, or patient?

I've always believed that before your 20s you learn your lessons, in your 20s you pay your dues, in your 30s you do your own thing, in your 40s and 50s (the high income producing years) you exploit what you know, and in your 60s and beyond, you share it. But you should never stop learning. And to get a job, you have to know what careers appeal to you.

Being good with words is always a good thing. One director of European operations graduated from college with a degree in electrical engineering but began to get jobs as a freelance technical writer when he realized that he liked talking about engineering better than he liked doing it. "Because engineers and marketers don't speak the same language," he reports, "I became the tech guys' translator for speeches, ad copy, journals and press releases.

But before you pursue a career solely in communications, be sure that you have something to communicate. It was some of the best advice my father ever gave me. His colleagues' kids were getting out of the prestigious j-schools (journalism) with no background in anything else to report on.

There are only so many people who can cover the subject of "breaking news," and it takes a long time to get there. In the meantime, it's helpful to have a second major, a minor, even a hobby or a sport in which you excel or have specialized knowledge to report on in landing a job in communications.

And spell check, spell check, spell check! Resumes with even one typo get no response from most employers.

The Interview

Being a little early and immaculately dressed and groomed shows your respect for the position and the people as well as your desire to get the job. Make it your goal to be offered every job you apply for so you can pick and choose.

Sit where and when you are invited to do so. Don't wait till you are in the lobby to read the annual report. All of your homework should have been done online from home. But if there is an interesting reprint or article about the company in the lobby, you know they are proud of it and may be a good conversation starter once the interview begins.

Accept a beverage if you are offered one, use a coaster or napkin if provided, and do not litter the office by not at least making a gesture of carrying the can or cup out with you.

According to manners maven Marjabelle Young Stewart, 90 percent of success in an initial job interview is how you present yourself. "Be polite to everyone you meet. The receptionist may be as responsive to you as a light fixture, but she may also be a spy for the interviewer. She can report back that you were (a) extremely congenial or (b) rather snobbish, brash, or whatever else, and this might cost you the job."

Unless you're independently wealthy, about the only way to avoid the occasional round of job interviews is to go into business for yourself. As a long-time entrepreneur, I will tell you that that may be overreacting.

It is estimated that in the 40 to 45 years between graduation and retirement, we will each have, on average, five different careers. So knowing how to present yourself to your best advantage to a potential employer is very important.

Look at the process as a way of networking within your industry.

Do what you can to not be too desperate or too cavalier about the job. Employers are people too, and want their opportunity to be valued, but not as a last resort. So stop yourself before you get too discouraged, depressed, or desperate. To paraphrase an old saying, when the employee is ready, the job will come. So, continue to prepare yourself with more education, skills, industry-specific information, and knowledge of trends.

One job applicant I coached had a brand spanking new MBA but not a clue where to get a job. I assigned him the task of choosing three industries that interested him or he had some background in. He was to research and read each industry's trade publications, attend industry functions, and be prepared to explain to an interviewer why the industry, company, product, or service was a good fit for him.

Learn as much as you can to ask intelligent questions of genuine interest to you. But don't try to impress the interviewer with your knowledge. Presumably, he or she will know much more.

Every resume has a few Achilles heels. Have you never worked in this industry before? Was there a long stretch of time that you were out of work? Might you seem too much of a dinosaur because you were working in the industry before your interviewer was even born? This was the case for one entertainment industry applicant, so we dropped his early experience on TV shows that were too old to remember in favor of more details of his experience on recent shows.

A wheelchair-bound client added humor to her rap by saying that she first wanted to be a dance instructor, but decided instead to use her God-given talent in computers. Since she could type 121 words a minute, she never looked back.

In another case history, a client was very proud of his name, Mohammad, but acknowledged that it had been impossible for him to land a new job after 9/11. We coached him to mention his Middle Eastern background and explain how it had propelled him to attend a very prestigious graduate school in the United States for his MBA.

If your resume contains a topic that might be considered a "pink elephant," address it to open the subject for discussion, if necessary. More often than not, a simple comment bridged to a related benefit will be more than enough to dispel the issue. And you may well hear your interviewer using your explanation in presenting you to his or her peers.

Some industry executives will spend time with you, even if there is no position currently available. Take this opportunity because every industry is a small town and you never know who knows whom. Avoid the phrase "pick your brain," which is not a very appealing word picture for the victim. Still, learning what you can both before the interview and during it, will make you that much savvier in the next one.

Helping to produce Regis Philbin's *AM Los Angeles*, I will never forget how many wannabes interviewed to be interns without ever having even watched the show. They just knew they wanted to work in television. "But how much help would they be?" we asked ourselves.

Avoid cattiness at all costs, but be ready to hear the insider gossip. Let it roll off your back without being judgmental or condescending. And never, never, never repeat it. You never know where alliances lie.

Conferencing

Reading maketh a full man, conference a ready man, and writing an exact man.

—Francis Bacon

If conference makes a ready man, then teleconferencing and videoconferencing should make him ready that much more efficiently. Surprisingly, although the technology of audio- and videoconferencing has existed for almost the last two decades, it has been painfully slow in catching on.

Some speculate that participants are justifiably self-conscious on camera or miss the opportunity to travel far and worldwide to make contacts in person. Perhaps, like so many things, that has changed post 9/11.

To wit, the quarterly audio conference calls required by every public company includes hundreds of industry and financial analysts, the press and stockholders in both one- and two-way conversations with CEOs and CFOs.

Despite its popularity, or lack thereof, technology marches on. The conference table videoconference may soon give way to the individual camera at desk or laptop or cell phone. Perhaps, much as it took the personal computer to revolutionize computing, it will take desktop-mounted cameras or individual cell phones to revolutionize audio- and videoconferencing.

Always at the forefront of putting technology to work, Intel recommends implementing technological tools to make meetings easier. The emphasis on teamwork in today's workplace has created a movement towards implementing collaborative technology in the meeting room. This technology includes computers, LCD projectors, and interactive whiteboards. Employing these technologies will allow meeting participants to access computer-based information, share data, and automatically save information generated during their meetings—all functionality for enhanced group collaboration.

Desktops and Laptops

With desktop and laptop computers, as in other areas of business, technology is helping make meetings easier and more efficient. In many organizations today, e-mail is being used as a quick and easy method of communicating information internally without the need for meeting. In fact, four out of five executives share meeting notes with colleagues—three-quarters of them by e-mail. However, even with the help of e-mail to communicate, nearly half of the executives polled still feel overwhelmed by the number of meetings they attend. This indicates that technology is helping today's meeting dilemma, but not entirely solving it.

Videoconferencing

As Walt Kelly penned in his Pogo cartoon series years ago, "We have met the enemy, and he is us." Whether audio- or videoconferencing, or a meeting in person, the technology is only as good as the people who run it.

Since the technology does exist, many global companies are still trying to adopt videoconferencing to communicate across distances. In 1996, manufacturers shipped approximately 300,000 systems and by 1997, nearly 1.4 million copies of videoconferencing software were loaded onto PCs across America. Given the need for fast communication in today's workplace, the cost in time and energy of international travel to communicate over distances and the increase in the number of meetings to facilitate team-based decision-making, many organizations say that they would like to implement videoconferencing as a common meeting practice.

Glen Miller, the director of worldwide video and satellite communications for Pharmacia Upjohn, has installed enterprise-wide videoconferencing equipment and witnessed the benefits of this technology. "The ability to interact with others remotely produces huge corporate benefits," says Miller. "Last year, for example, videoconferencing slashed more than $6 million in direct travel expenses for Pharmacia Upjohn. It also freed up about 2,000 workdays that managers and executives used to spend in transit."

The challenge, as always, is to communicate, learn, and commit to the techniques and technology that will improve conferencing, a technologically enhanced meeting.

The Peter Principle

Like people, following the Peter Principle, every meeting seems to rise to its own level of incompetence. Individuals bring such different perspectives to the table in meetings that communication is much more confused than we tend to think. Whether you're responsible for the budget, production, bucking for a promotion, fearing you'll be fired, or distracted by other things going on in your life, you hear and speak through a filter of personal agenda.

If it's your job to move the group toward a solution or your point of view, you must lead different minds with different agendas as well as what George David Kieffer in his book *The Strategy of Meetings*, calls the group mind. He adds that if someone in the group is intent on defeating your purpose or simply disagrees with you, it's harder still.

When it comes to the group mind, says Kieffer, the whole can sometimes be less than the sum of the parts. Much less. And surprisingly, decisions made by the group can be riskier than any of the individuals would make on his or her own. This is thought to be a result of either the fact that there is less responsibility by each individual for the decision or that risk-prone individuals seem to dominate meetings.

A fight-or-flight mentality exists for many in meetings and it seems to be compounded by how long the meeting lasts, which is typically too long. There is a law of diminishing returns in most meetings and the good meeting manager knows and reads it. If 80 percent of the results are accomplished in 20 percent of the time, why go on?

A meeting should not be your first line of defense or solution; it should be your final one. Because meetings are so fraught with peril as a waster of time, talent, money, motivation, and reputation, proceed with caution! Remember that less and fewer are more.

Follow the Leader

Whether you called the meeting or not, your boss is there or isn't, Kieffer argues that every meeting is "your" meeting. As a participant, you must participate in achieving the best result. In rowing, the coxswain calls the strokes, but every rower pulls her own oar.

And more than in any other sport, except perhaps for meetings, the experiences of coxswaining and rowing are altogether different from each other. You're each in a different battle in the same war. Your objectives may be different, but your responsibility to win is the same.

You can win the point and influence people by contributing to not only the substance of the meeting but to its spirit.

Meeting Is the Message

For Kieffer, a meeting is a medium, and in the famous words of Marshall McLuhan, "The medium is the message. That is to say, the way we acquire information affects us more than the information itself." A meeting, again in McLuhan's words, "does something to people; it takes hold of them, bumps them around."

Thus the manner can affect the participants and the organization more than the material. As we saw from that very popular television show, *Survivor*. Who needs whom? What alliances will help you succeed or fail?

The now-popular phrase, "herding cats," is operative in meetings. Unlike horses or cattle, people seem to be averse to going in a direction together. The journey of a thousand miles may begin with a single step, but not if everyone is stepping in different directions.

You must separate the **process** from the **purpose**, the **problems**, and the **people**. What process will favor your agenda or solution? Fight for that first.

Any problem-solution process begins with the complaint, the history, its perspective in light of other complaints, the diagnosis, and the prescription for cure.

Make sure that all of the decision-makers in your meeting are beginning together on the task at hand. If not everyone is in agreement or can be persuaded about the purpose of a meeting, you are going to fail in getting to a conclusion.

One of Stephen Covey's habits of highly successful people is to begin with the end in mind. Meetings, in contrast to any good story, often have a beginning, a *muddle*, and an end. A muddle means getting mired in the middle with no light at the end of the tunnel. It is best prevented by frequently taking the temperature of the room. Is it hot or cold? On track or off? To what degree are we cooking towards a solution? If the discussion seems disorganized, go back and redefine your purpose.

When it comes to people: Who will become defensive? Who will align themselves together? Who will bully? Who will zone out?

There always seems to be a fly in the ointment of every meeting. Sometimes, more than one. Picture him, stuck there, but not going quietly. His strength, resolve, and fight may make him a squadron leader if you can get him unstuck and position him correctly to channel his energy more positively.

Be on purpose; understand that a meeting is a means to an end like a decision or a solution. Seldom the end in and of itself.

The following is from Intel's basic principles of effective meetings class materials and should be applied to your own tele- and videoconferencing.

■   ■   ■   ■   ■

The basic principles of effective meetings at Intel include meeting types; roles and responsibilities; meeting behaviors; and meeting preparation and follow-up. Topics include mission and process meetings; agendas; meeting minutes; diverse meeting participants, and geographically dispersed meeting issues.

The goal of this course is to build competence in one of Intel's core business practices. Participants will more fully understand the importance of meetings and will learn skills for preparing for—and participating in—meetings back on the job.

- Distinguish between process meetings and mission meetings.

- Identify the six rules for an effective agenda.
- Operate in the key meeting roles.
- Describe the use of meeting tools and tips, such as scheduling, teleconferencing, and meeting minutes.
- Define considerations necessary to holding effective meetings with diverse participants and geographically dispersed teams.

It is important to be sensitive to differences among participants from diverse backgrounds and cultures. You might discuss how styles of meeting participation could vary among team members from different groups or countries. Consider what it means to hold meetings with respect and trust, and to listen to all ideas and viewpoints in groups of diverse participants.

You have the foundation for an effective meeting when you can answer the following:

- *Do you know the purpose of the meeting?*
- *Do you have an agenda?*
- *Do you know your role and are you prepared?*
- *Do you know how and to whom the results will be communicated?*

TWO TYPES OF MEETINGS

There are two basic types of meetings at Intel; each type has a different purpose:

- Process meetings
- Mission meetings

When meetings get off-track, it is usually because we have lost sight of which type of meeting we are in—or we have mistakenly jumped from one type to the other. It is your responsibility to know which type of meeting you are in, and to prepare and participate accordingly.

Process Meetings	Mission Meetings
Regular	As needed
Sustain organizational structure and processes	Leverage group intelligence to accomplish a specific result
Ratify or veto proposals	Solve problems
Make decisions	Make recommendations
Share or update information	Accomplish a deliverable
Allocate resources	Plan a project
Reflects the organization—all who need to know	Relevant and necessary to accomplish the task—generally 5-6 individuals
Business Update Meeting (BUM)	Task team
Staff Meeting	Project team
1:1s with manager (could become Mission meeting)	Development team

AGENDAS

An effective meeting agenda:

- enables participants to come to the meeting prepared
- gives meeting participants a framework to follow in accomplishing the goals of the meeting in the time allowed.

Agendas might be sent via email; they might also be posted on share drives, in eRooms, or using Web Meeting Manager. It is your responsibility to review the agenda and come prepared to contribute to the outcome of each agenda item.

Rule 1: Separate Items

Keep the various types of meeting work separate. At the very least, separate mission and process sections of the agenda. Keep agenda items separate within in each section, along with WHO will present, and the PROCESS for addressing that topic.

Rule 2: Estimate Time Frames

Schedule amount of time for each item, even if an estimate. END the meeting at 10 minutes before the hour.

Rule 3: List Attendees

List who is expected to attend the meeting. The guiding principle for meeting attendance: ONLY those relevant to the agenda.

Rule 4: Pre-publish

Pre-publish the agenda (1-5 working days in advance, keeping in mind various time zones). Attach appropriate documents, or inform participants where the documents are located (e.g., an eRoom or Web Meeting Manager). Note if NetMeeting will be used, so they can plan accordingly.

Rule 5: Clarify Decision Method (at least in the first team meeting)

Clarify the method for making decisions (i.e., consultative, consensus, authoritative, voting) BEFORE the meeting begins.

Rule 6: Clarify Expected Outcomes

Clarify expected outcome for each agenda item. Screen potential topics to ensure that they are relevant, important, and appropriate for the meeting.

Meeting Roles

Overview   Having defined meeting roles makes a meeting more effective by clearly laying out expectations. If someone is designated to take notes (Recorder) or invite participation (Gatekeeper), meeting participants will move agenda items toward their expected outcomes. The meeting leader might assign roles ahead of time, or the assignments might be done at the start of the meeting.

Following are the essential meeting roles:

Facilitator
- Drives the meeting process.
- Ensures that outcomes are reached by focusing on the effectiveness of the group process.
- Assigns other 'helping' roles, when needed, such as a NetMeeting facilitator to coordinate presentations.

Timekeeper
- Keeps the group aware of time passage to check against time allotted for the task.
- Helps keep the participants on designated agenda times.

Recorder (Scribe)
- Provides group memory for all to see (if the meeting is face-to-face, in one conference room).
- Documents meeting summary, decisions, ARs, bin list items, and next steps.
- Might also publish minutes.

Gatekeeper
- Invites silent members to speak, or discourages those who talk too much. Example: "Carlos, you have experience in this type of activity. What is your opinion on the direction we are taking?"

Scheduling Meetings

Geo-Dispersed meeting challenges
With many employees working on geographically dispersed teams, early and thorough preparation is even more crucial, especially when the participants are in different locations around the world.

Time Considerations
When participants are located in different time zones, this can limit your window of opportunity for meetings. Consider the following when scheduling meetings:

- Time zones, weekends, national holidays
- Some groups meet this challenge by:
  - Rotating meeting times to share the pain
  - Structuring sub-groups or task groups so that the members are within closer time zones, where possible
  - Doing their non-urgent work in an eRoom, and holding meetings less frequently.

Culture and Other Dimensions of Diversity

Meeting style can be very different for people from different personal backgrounds and cultures. In diverse groups it helps to take into consideration the differences among participants, and to learn about each other's varied approaches.

Telephone Bridges

If you are responsible for scheduling a phone meeting:

- Follow Intel's bridge-scheduling process.

Publish the dial-in number, reservation, and passcode on your meeting invitation *and* agenda.

Conference Rooms

If some of the meeting participants will be in conference rooms, be sure to list conference rooms at each site, with seating capacity and phone numbers.

(Reprinted by permission of Intel Corporation.)

Panels, Seminars, Workshops, and Conferences

...and knoweth not who shall gather them.
—Psalms 39:6

In this information age, one of the most efficient ways to learn is to be briefed by experts in the field at a panel discussion, seminar, or workshop. The raw data has been researched, cultivated, processed, experimented with, and edited down to simply what you need to know. The number of presenters, the length of the training, and the depth of audience involvement defines the vehicle for learning.

Panels

For an event organizer, a panel of speakers offers the challenge of booking a moderator and three or four speakers instead of one. But it's a good investment of time and energy. Because each speaker will interest a different segment, there will probably be a bigger audience. And all the speakers should be encouraged to invite their friends, clients, and business associates to hear them speak.

In the nonprofit sector, such as universities, a panel provides an opportunity for the same information to be presented from different points of view. And even in an academic arena, likeability and making it an enjoyable learning experience instead of a boring lecture go a long way in creating a professional reputation.

A panel takes pressure off the speakers to be brilliant and to hold the attention of the entire audience for the evening or afternoon. You will endear yourself to a program chair if you can suggest other speakers to be on a panel with you. And, usually, your friends, the other speakers, will be complimented as well. By suggesting a vertical rather than horizontal panel, you can avoid direct competitors and select your contractors or, better yet, a client, to speak on the topic or be the moderator. For additional visibility, you may offer to be both a speaker and moderator. In this case, you must bend over backwards to give every speaker his or her due and not hog the podium or microphone.

If you suggest the panel, work with the program chair to make it a timely and provocative topic that will elicit a lot of interest. And suggest a lineup that makes logical sense.

If your panel is already selected, learn ahead of time from the chair or moderator who each speaker is and in what order the panelists will speak. Ask in what position you will bat— first, second, third, or clean-up. Chances are, your moderator hasn't definitely decided yet and you may get to choose. Once again, have in mind a logical sequence, featuring your choice. I prefer second. By that time, the audience is warmed up, they haven't tired of listening, and everything you want to say hasn't already been said. If you know that one of the panelists is an exceptionally good speaker, try to come before, not immediately after, her.

Whatever the order, take the time to research the bios and backgrounds of the other panelists and be generous in spirit, even if they are your biggest competitors. A panel is a great opportunity for potential customers to compare and contrast the competition and you want to appear gracious and good-natured. Acting as the winner helps to ensure that you will be!

Take a dynamic point of view, but not one that contradicts your business philosophy. Address the topic both from experience and research. Learn something new about the subject because an interested speaker is a more interesting one. The audience will think it is only the tip of the iceberg of what you know.

As a panelist or in any speaking situation, be subtle in your advertising or self-promotion. Use your experience, client list, or case histories as logical examples of points that need to be made. Avoid being too commercial. This isn't a new business pitch. Your authority is already acknowledged by being there and a captive audience will squirm like a moth on a pin if they have to listen to a sales pitch.

Once the topic and panel are established, work again with the organizer or chair to get your bio and picture into her hands. And mail or e-mail the promotional piece or flyer out to everyone you know or want to know. As with any party, it's not who comes but who gets invited that counts.

Again, you will endear yourself to the organizers who are always scrambling to fill the audience. Depending on your or your company's resources, the panel participants, and the organization, you may want to buy a table for associates and/or clients.

As a panelist, you should not have waited until the other panelists are speaking to be writing your part of the presentation. Instead, look intently at each speaker and listen very carefully to what each one says, noting places where you can refer back for agreement. Very often the audience will be watching you to see how interested you are in what the others have to say. Nothing will hurt the others' credibility or yours more than a yawn from you or a roll of your eyes or even staring into space.

As a moderator, you are the team leader and need to make sure everyone is on the same page regarding blocking, how long each presentation should be, what aspects of the topic each should address, and whether they should stand at the podium or sit at their places with table mikes. I recommend that the presenters use the podium for their presentations in order to give each individual recognition, and then take a team approach to answering questions on table mikes.

If you can do it subtly, take your position at the end of the table, stage right, audience left. It is the power position because an audience reads the front of a room like they read a newspaper, and their eyes keep returning to the left. Often the bookends hold the stage during the Q&A and the middle players end up looking like they are watching a tennis match between two really good players.

Seminars

Merriam-Webster's Dictionary defines the seminar as a supervised session or course for advanced study. But seminars don't have to be just one-way conversations with only facial expressions or body language for feedback. They should be very interactive.

Every audience has smilers and stoics. Both can be misleading. Smilers will smile and nod at anything, that's their social mode. Involve the stoics and those who are looking at their shoes. Interrupt your flow and engage the stoic with questions. "Bill?" (it's on his name tag). "May I call you, Bill?" (reluctant agreement). "Bill, based on your experience, would you choose A or B?" (both are correct and everyone knows it). Hire fewer people and pay them more or pay less and be able to hire more people? Layoffs. Salary. Telegraph the answer. Ask another, "John, would you go with that? To keep things moving, let's pretend that you do...."

Workshops

What distinguishes a workshop from a panel and seminar is that in a workshop, performance is required. Workshops are centered on performance and testing. It is an English translation of the French word *atelier*, apprenticing to a master.

In a workshop, the organizer must first be able to assess existing skill levels in each participant. At Ready for Media, we do this with an assessment by the organizer and a short, concise pre-questionnaire to each of the participants that includes questions about past experience in media and speaking situations, the image they believe their companies, products, and they themselves have and what they hope to accomplish. Filling out a questionnaire in advance has the added advantage of helping each participant begin to focus on the upcoming workshop, think about what they want or need to learn, and provide individual "buy-in" from each.

Secondly, the material to be learned must be organized psychologically rather than logically for use. This means organization according to "ease of learning." For example, by geographical desirability or experience level may be more important to you than organization by alphabet or numerically.

Thirdly, you must present enabling steps, with an opportunity for participants to fail in absolute safety. We do this with a great amount of humor and sometimes the participants' help. I'll never forget the CEO who requested gin and chocolate as her snacks of choice. Naturally, we had a miniature bottle of Bombay and a box of chocolates waiting for her and it became the running joke throughout the day.

And, finally, there must be an opportunity to try/test what participants are learning and see their progress. There is magic

in self-improvement. The participants have challenged themselves and won, and that makes everyone very happy.

The participants are your gold. All you need to do is mine
them. As a woman, I can good-naturedly tease the audience,
while male workshop leaders tell me their secret is be jocular.

Throughout, you must be vigilant that your participants are
protected. You are asking them to leave their egos at the door,
kind of like a crab that sheds his shell to grow. While they are
soft and vulnerable, you must protect them, both from their
own self-critique and from each others'.

One workshop leader tells the story of noticing that one of
his workshop participants was in tears after a particularly difficult exercise. He casually stood by her as he proceeded with
his explanation of the next point and then asked if anyone had a
tissue. There were five offers. Then he calmly asked her if she
would prefer an answer to a question or a hug. Sniffling, she
chose a hug, and he asked who in the room could give her a
hug. Everyone offered.

Conferences

Worldwide gatherings of an industry or specialty keep participants from around the world up to date on research, findings,
and the state of the art. As a former journalist, I am increasingly
being asked to function as a conference moderator. Apparently,
a lively interview with one or more participants is replacing
days of dry, dull, overly detailed technical presentations.

Introductions

I wish I loved the Human Race;
I wish I loved its silly face:
I wish I liked the way it walks;
I wish I liked the way it talks:
And when I'm introduced to one
I wish I thought What Jolly Fun!

—Sir Walter Raleigh, "Wishes of an Elderly Man
Wished at a Garden Party, June 1914"

In making business introductions, the oldest or most senior person is addressed first. Despite Sir Raleigh, think of it as an important courtesy not to let him or her stand there without knowing to whom he is speaking.

"Mr. L, I'd like you to meet our new Manager of Client and Media Relations, Olivia Burtis." Then offer something of interest as a conversation starter to the senior person, such as "Mr. L, Olivia went to Stanford, too." Or "Mr. L, Olivia has just received her MBA from UCLA's Anderson School." Or give the junior person an opening to make conversation with your client by suggesting, "Olivia, Mr. L plans for us to coach his clients all over the world. You can use your Italian."

When you are in a social setting or you are coupled, a woman is always addressed first. Guests, unless they are elderly or dignitaries, are presented to a host or hostess as well as to the guest of honor. Designations such as Doctor (M.D. or Ph.D.), Lieutenant, General, Mayor, Governor, Judge, Pastor, or Reverend should be included unless you know that the individual prefers that it not be. In a self-introduction, give your first name (the way you wish to be addressed) and last name, deleting the titles.

Meeting someone for the first time, look for commonalities with which to relate. The situation, location, weather, or even traffic may be a good conversation starter. Other commonalities may include geography, alma maters, and hobbies.

Networking

If meeting and greeting is new to you, practice, practice, practice meeting people and making friends. Increasingly, networking is used for prospecting for new clients, establishing a presence in your industry, and getting the word out about a new or improved product or service. It is probably the most cost-effective marketing tool a company can employ. Both personally and professionally, it's often not what you know but who that makes all the difference.

As a host or hostess, it's your job to introduce people to each other, preferably with some clue to a common interest that they will find interesting to talk about. Sometimes, just introducing each one with a title or area of expertise gives them a starting point. When I host a party, I will often put someone else's name on the back of a name tag and a two or three word identifier (avid golfer) so people will be seeking each other out.

In introducing one person or a guest of honor to many, as long as everyone is acknowledged, all of the names are less important (it's why you have name tags) than what brings you all together.

In introducing a speaker, look for the unique and different but applicable things in a speaker's background that will intrigue an audience. If you are the speaker, give your host some ammunition to make your audience look forward to what you have to say. Begin with, "It's a little known fact that...." And even after you've been introduced as a speaker, drop a few names or experiences into your conversation or speech to keep the audience interested. Chances are the audience wasn't paying much attention until you grabbed their attention and made sure they were listening to WII-FM, all together now, "What's In It For Me?"

At a no-host event, not only do you have to pay for your own wine but you're on your own when it comes to introductions, too. Being well-informed on current events, movies, museum exhibits, and sporting events provides good conversation starters. Another technique is to encourage others to talk about themselves and be good listeners. That involves asking thoughtful follow-up questions until you really understand. One of Stephen Covey's *7 Habits of Highly Successful People* is to understand before you seek to be understood.

Exiting a conversation is a matter of simply asking to be excused. Asking for a card if you would like to stay in touch is a gracious way to bring a conversation to a close. On a plane, when you may be a captive audience for several hours, it is perfectly acceptable to bury your nose in a book after acknowledging your seat mate, but you may be missing a lot.

The Sweetest Sound

In polite conversation, it is appropriate to mention the person's first name at the end of the conversation, particularly by phone. Since his name is probably his favorite or at least the most familiar word in all the world to him, make it part of your signoff or a gracious goodbye.

Media Interviews

The medium is the message.

— Marshall McLuhan

And the reporter's are your messengers. Letting the media tell your story, or at least your side of it, is the best way to make the most of limited resources. Think of all the writing talent and broadcasting resources that are beating a path to your door, if only you can get your thoughts together in support of your premise and give a good sound bite. Take a public interest viewpoint, and communicate it in clear, compelling, and concise answers.

In writing a recent article for an association of in-house counsel, or corporate attorneys, I reported on a panel of their peers who told them, in no uncertain terms to "'Just Say No' to 'No Comment.'" The reporters will tell the story with or without you. But journalists want a balanced story, if you will just give them that chance. If you stonewall them by expressing no defensible position or any position at all, you've made the story one-sided.

A press conference is a meeting, too. And not unlike most meetings, press conferences used to happen far too often. Publicists believed that if they scheduled a press conference, their announcements would seem important, too. Sometimes, on a slow news day, this works. But often, the media is too savvy and too busy with breaking news. Still, if you are a news-maker and you understand the news cycle by scheduling an announcement just before the media's deadlines, you can often create a story where none existed before.

One of the most poignant examples of using the media as a communications tool happened during the George W. Bush administration when Secretary of Defense Donald Rumsfeld suggested to a newly liberated Iraqi people to speak freely to the hundreds of imbedded journalists from around the world. To paraphrase him: Tell your stories of repression and torture under Sadam Hussein. Who better to help justify a war of liberation than the citizens it liberated? Asking Iraqi citizens to be media spokespeople used Marshall McLuhan's tenet, "The medium is the message" to perfection.

Although John F. Kennedy seemed a natural for the medium, President Nixon wasn't. "I was not lying," he explained. "I said things that later on seemed to be untrue."

It was the perfect example of denying negatives instead of professing positives. To a similar question, President Ronald Reagan began his answer with, "I believe in the integrity of the American people."

This law of communications once prompted me to ask my tennis instructor to please stop criticizing what I was doing wrong. "Don't take your eye off the ball." "Don't just stand there." "Don't toss the ball so high."

By calling my bad habits across the net, he was reinforcing my mistakes. Instead, I asked him to correct me with the proper technique. "Keep your eye on the ball." "Move your feet." "Toss the ball so you can hit it." My tennis game improved immeasurably. Finally, I heard what to do and could act on it.

The media has been a thorn in the side of many presidents and presidential hopefuls since the early days of television. In the first televised presidential debates, Richard Nixon's nerves, pallor, and 5 o'clock shadow contrasted sharply with the tan, relaxed, Jack Kennedy. And President Carter didn't fare much better in his November 1976 *Playboy* interview when he admitted that he "lusted in his heart." Asked about his religious beliefs, Carter replied not in a sound bite but in more a stream of consciousness:

> Christ said, I tell you that anyone who looks on a woman with lust has in his heart already committed adultery. I've looked on a lot of women with lust. I've committed adultery in my heart many times. This is something that God recognizes I will do—and I have done it— and God forgives me for it. But that doesn't mean that I condemn someone who not only looks on a woman with lust but who leaves his wife and shacks up with somebody out of wedlock. Christ says, Don't consider yourself better than someone else because one guy screws a whole bunch of women while the other guy is loyal to his wife.

God may have forgiven him but the public never forgave nor forgot, despite years and untold acts of kindness since.

Even the era of the first Bush White House garnered some classic quotes such as, "Well, on the manhood thing, I'll put mine against his, anytime," in response to his opponent Walter Mondale's challenge of, "He [George Bush] doesn't have the manhood to apologize."

George Bush's vice president, Dan Quayle, stepped into it too, with such statements as "Verbosity leads to unclear, inarticulate things." Referring to the Negro Colleges slogan, "A mind is a terrible thing to waste," Vice President Quayle was quoted as saying, "What a waste it is to lose one's mind or not to have a mind. How true that is." Later, the media further attributed to him, "I stand by all my misstatements."

Spontaneity can, and must, be learned, particularly when your shots will be heard round the world. It is generally thought that such presidential hopefuls as Dan Quayle, Al Gore, and Bob Dole lost their presidential bids in the media.

It helped such a practiced performer as Ronald Reagan win his. "There you go," was a famous non-answer. He was legendary for his shoebox full of cards, with an idea on each one of what people wanted to hear: an actor with his own lines.

George W. Bush's 21st century administration has come a long way in understanding the old saw, if you can't beat 'em, join 'em. Although many speculated at the tradeoffs in the name of security that the network news organizations may have made for having military access to the war in Iraq, the Bush administration seemed to understand that no one could or would tell the story as well as the media. There seemed to be an appreciation of each other's role in the process. Corporations should take note in letting the media work for, not *against*, them.

Media Mistakes Not to Make

Politically incorrect, culturally insensitive, last-minute remarks made in anger or jest can get anyone fired, or worse. Distinguished careers are forgotten in an instant, replaced by a sound bite that lives on forever. These are just some examples, including infamous quotes from sports stars, politicians, and celebrities culled over the last two decades from Ready for Media's well-loved library of Media Mistakes Not to Make.

One, made in anger and frustration by President Clinton's secretary of the interior, Bruce Babbitt, as he pulled the lavaliere microphone from his chest and tossed it on the floor, was used all weekend to promote the ABC program *John Stossel Goes to Washington*. "I'm going to fire whoever scheduled this interview." Poignant to this day because it no doubt strikes terror into the hearts and minds of everyone who has a boss or an important client.

Don't try to find sound bites or lines. Sound bites will come naturally when, like Winston Churchill, you speak a simple truth, "The maxim of the British people is 'Business as usual'" or offer a powerful word picture, "An iron curtain has descended across the continent."

Gotcha Game

Critics blame media for the *Gotcha Game*, society's newly popular sport, but when spokespeople say the stupidest things, what's a waiting media to do? There are just too many column inches and broadcast minutes to fill. Besides, it's their job!

The secret is, don't be surprised. Think about what you want to say on the way there and don't be caught speaking without thinking.

Former Senate Majority Leader Trent Lott apparently spoke without thinking on December 5, 2002. What goes around, comes around, they say. And it comes and goes, really fast. By mid December, *The Boston Globe* quoted an aide as saying that the Mississippi senator was in the habit of arriving at meetings unprepared, as he apparently did at Strom Thurmond's 100th birthday party celebration on that fateful December day. There, Mr. Lott noted that his state had supported the renegade centenarian's 1948 Segregationist bid for the Oval Office. According to the gentleman from Mississippi, if the rest of the nation had simply followed his state's lead, "we wouldn't have had all these problems over all these years." Less than a month later, the off-hand and presumably cordial attempt at jocularity with an old friend and fellow senator lost Mr. Lott the respect of many and his lofty Senate position as well.

And media mistakes are not reserved for inside the beltway. A press aide for Chicago's original Mayor Richard Daley, Sr., once pleaded, "You reporters should have reported what he meant, not what he said."

A National Rifle Association spokesperson was once quoted as making a case for guns with "[A gun is] a recreational tool, like a golf club or a tennis racket. You can kill someone with a golf club, you know!"

Chicago Cubs manager Jim Riggelman, was quoted as saying, " I try to have respect for people in general. Whether it's baseball players or lowlifes like the media." Atlanta Braves pitcher John Rocker was not New York's most valuable player when he pondered out loud the prospect of ever pitching for a New York team, "Imagine having to take the Number 7 [train] to the ballpark, looking like you're [riding through] Beirut next to some kid with purple hair next to some queer with AIDS right next to some dude who just got out of jail for the fourth time right next to some 20-year-old mom with four kids. It's depressing [to be in New York]."

The sports world is famous for other infamous quotes and for seeming racial slurs by the likes of greats such as baseball's Al Campanis and odds-maker, Jimmy the Greek. Sports commentator Fuzzy Zoeller sacrificed not only his reputation but a reported multi-million dollar contract when he said about Tiger Wood's first win of the Masters, "That little boy is driving well and he's putting well. So...pat him on the back...say 'Congratulations and enjoy it.' And tell him not to serve fried chicken next year...or collard greens or whatever the hell they serve." Apparently, he was simply chiding the young black golf star, but out of context, which a sound bite always is, even teasing can be lethal to careers and reputations.

And corporations are not exempt either. One of the classic loose cannons for the media are disgruntled ex-employees and franchise owners, not unlike the McDonald's franchisees who traded memos back and forth that ended up in *Time Magazine*. To the question, "Why did McDonald's latest promotion bomb?" the answer came back, "It's the food, stupid."

You are too nice a person to let the *Gotcha Game* happen to you.

Up to the Minute

This is a phrase used by news organizations all over the world. And yet it is also what you must be, too, if there is a chance that, like an estimated one in four of us, your 15 minutes of fame will be documented by the print or broadcast media. We recommend that clients read or review several newspapers and magazines, preferably daily, but at least the morning before an interview. The interviewers are news folks, and if they didn't write the story, they probably pulled it off the wires. You've got to be up on the latest because they may ask for your comments.

The Bush administration's secretary of state, Colin Powell, thought to be a master of communication, exemplified the importance of being up to the minute on media coverage. The story goes that he was asked by an Iraqi journalist at the start of the Iraq war whether it was true or not that according to *Forbes Magazine*, only about 17 percent of young, college-age Americans could even find Iraq on a world map. A media-savvy secretary of state shot back, "That may be true, but the bad news for Iraq is that they are all young Marines."

Obviously, the secretary had read the article or at least heard the statistic beforehand and had time to prepare a ready response. When you are in a position of interest to the media, it helps if you know how to play their game.

The BIGGEST Media Mistake

Not mentioning the name of the sponsor, company, product, or book by name early and often is the biggest branding mistake made in the media. A close second is not including the advertising slogan or subtitle, once you know what you're selling. At my company, Ready for Media, we have not been selling media strategy and communications coaching but giving confidence, confidence in communication, since 1981.

Crisis

Crisis happens even to the best companies and there is a proven formula for responding to it: give an acknowledgement of compassion, a bottom-line sound bite message, appropriate history, repeat of the sound bite, and then the next step. Rightly or wrongly, companies and/or their products have gotten reputations exclusively for how they have handled crisis. Johnson & Johnson's Tylenol poisonings was textbook crisis communication, as contrasted to Union Carbide's Bhopal or Chevron's Alaska oil crisis or even, more recently, Teflon for its decades of toxicity. Johnson & Johnson acted quickly to address the issue and used its media moment to introduce Tylenol's tamper-proof packaging on the front page of every newspaper in the world.

On Occasion

For courage mounteth with occasion.

—William Shakespeare

It's been a long time since any U.S. president has written his own speech on the back of an envelope. The one that started with "Four score and seven…" would probably be changed by today's speech writer to "47 years ago, our ancestors...." A more colorful scribe might make it, "A generation and a half," or "The time it took for a mom and dad and their teenagers to grow up in this country." Another might write, "Seventeen years after the house was paid off...."

An Entertaining MC

*Hostesses who entertain much must make up
their parties as ministers make up their cabinets,
on grounds other than personal liking.*

—George Eliot (pseudonym of Marian Evans Cross)

The role of mistress or master of ceremonies (MC) is a
tricky one. On the one hand, your job is to keep things moving
along in an entertaining way. On the other, it's not about you. It
is much like the conductor of an orchestra who stands in front
but has nothing to play. He or she is simply instrumental in
making music with all the other instruments.

One actress I know was asked at the last minute to step in
as MC for a well-known actor who was supposedly stuck on a
movie location. She said yes, in part because she believed in
the charity but also hoped that this role would bring her some
new exposure in Hollywood.

Every bone in her performer's body wanted to disclaim the
12-year-old picture and bio the organizers of the award's luncheon
had quickly pulled from the Internet and copied on brightly
colored flyers as handouts! After making a conscious decision
to make her remarks about the charity rather than herself, she
said not a word about the picture nor remark on the no-show
MC who had gotten all the polished publicity while taking none
of the responsibility for showing up. In fact, throughout the
event, she refrained from talking about herself at all. As a result,
she did her job superbly, because the charity, not she, was
the star of the day. She knew she succeeded because she got
lots of kudos.

Also critical was her attention to the script. She had seen too
many actors vainly stumble over this kind of script without practice
or their reading glasses. So even though she had only received
the script the night before, she did not make the mistake

of "winging it." While everyone else in Hollywood was networking at the cocktail reception in the foyer outside, our MC sat behind the podium rewriting and rehearsing her script.

And then an interesting thing happened. The organizers were mindful that the luncheon event usually ran way over schedule. By the end, the only audience members left sitting were those who were too polite to leave. What could she do to make sure that the unscripted awardees would say their piece and move on? "I'll come up and hug anyone who goes overtime saying thank you," she good-naturedly threatened the audience.

It was a sweet gesture and certainly not an unappealing prospect coming from her. Throughout the next hour, everyone teased about talking until they got their hugs, but they were brief and to the point and the afternoon ended with a full house, ahead of schedule. The MC's hugs became the running joke through every acceptance speech, much as Jack Palance's one-armed push-up did in the 1996 Academy Awards.

Another time, a lawyer was asked to be the MC at her firm's weekend retreat. Again, it was an opportunity to be showcased. This time, in front of all the senior partners in the firm. She was naturally funny, but scared to death. To help her, we broke it into seven acts or sections like a television show, and wrote introductions and conclusions to each segment. We helped her use the audience and its idiosyncrasies as material, which is a good way of making it about them instead of you.

Props, Microphones, and PowerPoint

A sharp tongue is the only edge tool that grows keener with constant use.

—Washington Irving

Knowing the tools of the trade makes all the difference to your abilities as a pro.

Props

One client, a software programmer at Apple Computer, endeared himself to an audience by using an armload of toilet paper rolls to differentiate the necessary paperwork from the unnecessary his program would eliminate.

Illustrating points with props and pictures sometimes makes a personal story even better. A start-up client was to be one of 75 presenters/solicitors to a venture capitalist audience. In discussing the watershed moments of his life beforehand, I discovered that he had been an amateur hockey player. As his speech coach, I searched the sporting-goods stores the night before to find an actual hockey stick. On stage, he captivated the mostly male audience with tales of his hockey career and used the stick as a prop to illustrate the perfect *hockey stick curve* projection that every investor knows and loves. He became the "guy with the hockey stick" who got all the money because he was unique and memorable. In a word, fact is often better than fiction.

Once I used a box of Crayolas to help another client launch an entire industry. In the early days of color printers, there was an intense competition for the technology that would become the industry standard. Our client prided itself on a solid, wax process that, to me, resembled a crayon. In all the charts and graphs, colorful Crayolas represented our client with a lightning bolt for another company's laser process and a drop for the liquid one. The main point of the presentation, later trademarked as their advertising slogan, was *Color Goes To Work*. It adorned every sort of promotional item from T-shirts to mugs to baseball caps. For note-taking at huge product presentations, we created a briefcase-shaped coloring book with a small packet of Crayolas attached to the front. Many in our audiences, worldwide, asked for extras to take home to their kids!

Microphones

A hand-held mike or podium microphone is directional and need only point at the spoken sound. You should work the crook-neck on the podium to direct it directly at your mouth rather than bending over or contorting to speak into it. If the speaker before you is taller or shorter, practice adjusting it up or down before the audience comes in so it will be a natural adjustment to make when you begin speaking.

All too often, speakers are intimidated by the technology of microphones, the TelePrompTer, and even the podium light, and wait till they are speaking to find out what they don't know about the logistics. Technicians, as a rule, or at least the banquet captain, are usually more than happy to work with you, including dimming lights for slides. Dimming doesn't mean fading to complete darkness because it's too easy for an audience to fall asleep after wine and a big dinner or lunch when the lights go out.

Still, you must take the initiative to take the stage or walk up to the podium ahead of time. Look out at the room, get the feel of the size, shape, and set-up. Say a few words into the mike. Make sure the podium light works, and if it's not bright enough, bring your reading glasses.

If there's a TelePrompTer, is the screen on a camera in front of you or to the sides? Practice with the operator on your pacing. Enlist his or her expertise in which line to read, slowing you down, and marking the script for emphasis with underlining or spacing or color.

Ask, beforehand, that your podium be stage right/the audiences left if at all possible (it is the commanding position because English-speaking audience read the front of a room like a newspaper). Further, ask that the mike be able to be disconnected from the podium so you can leave the podium for questions or switch off the microphone and switch on a wireless hand mike to meet the audience for questions without a barrier between you. I prefer a wireless hand mike to a wireless lavaliere that is pinned on and usually works as well, but the hand mike gives me something to hold on to and makes me feel more like an entertainer who has her act together. Plus, everyone knows stories about people, even the most media-savvy U.S. president, who spoke without thinking that a microphone was on.

PowerPoint

Perhaps the greatest invention ever pioneered for putting a speaker in command of his destiny is Microsoft PowerPoint, which provides the capability to design and change your graphics at a moment's notice. Still you've got to do everything you can to make sure your PowerPoint presentation works for you. If possible, have someone there, following along in your script, whose sole responsibility it is to change the screens. Or change them yourself from your laptop on the podium while the audience watches the projection behind you. Just as you don't want to read the script, don't read the slides. Make your talking points simple phrases or bullet points, not sentences and paragraphs. Then use the bullet point in sentences so your audience knows where you are on the slide. As with the script, avoid making last minute PowerPoint changes that will confuse you or force you to read them because you don't know the material yet.

Depositions and Testimony

No testimony is sufficient to establish a miracle.

—David Hume

In depositions, the emphasis is on a few words. As few as possible. Most lawyers will tell you to just answer the question and not offer any more. Yes and no are very often the place to both start and stop. In other words, don't volunteer or be colorful in your descriptions. And remember that the stenographer doesn't take notes until you begin speaking. So be natural, but you can take a moment to edit yourself before you begin speaking.

It is often said that lawyers never ask questions to which they don't think they already have the answers. Don't surprise your lawyer or help the other side at a deposition or trial by adding things that your lawyer is not expecting. The time to share with your attorney is before you get to the testimony so he or she can accurately make your case.

If you don't follow this advice, you may be guilty of hanging yourself with too much rope of too many words.

New Business Pitches and Product Presentations

Thou art not for the fashion of these times,
Where none will sweat but for promotion.

—William Shakespeare

The close. The courage to ask for the order. The client expects it. As George David Kieffer points out, "You can't fear the no, it's part of the asking." Not only will the impression you make be much worse if you never ask, you won't get a clear yes either.

The audience is never more crucial than in a new business or sales pitch. The more accurately you can determine the client's true needs, the more likely you are to make the sale.

One director of corporate communications who was interviewing Ready for Media for speech coaching confided that she looked like she was failing at her job because of the way her boss gave briefings or remarks. He was convinced that he was boring and had nothing to offer an audience. Instead of giving her the days and weeks she needed to craft a good speech and himself the time to practice, he avoided it until the very last minute, then asked her to come up with something.

In the perfect self-fulfilling prophecy, he read her hastily written words and he was boring, with nothing much to offer an audience. Once we learned why we were important to her, we had a much better chance of selling her a contract with us.

Very often, however, potential clients tell you what they think they want in either a product or a service. They either aren't aware of what their true needs are or they feel too vulnerable to let you in on them.

In a technique called Need-Benefit Selling, you need to discover the real needs and answer them with benefits.

Begin with active listening by assigning emotions to the wants. For example, when someone gives me a laundry list of wants, I answer with one or more emotions, such as frustration, embarrassment, mistrust, and disappointment, that the client must experience to make him want to make changes. If I've guessed wrong, the client will quickly correct me and we will begin to define the needs that he is experiencing.

Benefits are applied features. For example, a feature of my communications service is videotape feedback with constructive critique. Applying this feature as a benefit to the client means that Ready for Media's video capability allows the client to experience his speaking as the audience does. So if the client needs assurance that he is coming across well, the benefit is seeing himself as others see him.

List the features of your product, service, or self and translate them into benefits for your customers.

After defining several needs, answered by benefits, the client should have enough ammunition to convince herself that her needs will be answered by your product or service.

When a client is not forthcoming about his wants or needs, a general benefit statement is called for. This is also known as an "elevator pitch," because it should not take longer to present than it takes to go from the 25th floor, where you may get on the elevator with a potential new customer, to the lobby, where everyone gets off. For example, "Ready for Media is a communications coaching firm that lets you see yourself as your audiences see you, whether you are presenting yourself in person or through the media. We've been giving clients confidence in communication since 1981."

The most important thing in an elevator pitch is to translate the features into customer benefits. For example, where is the benefit to the potential client in learning that the home you wish to sell them has ocean views, four bedrooms, skylights, and a three-car garage? It's better to put them in the picture by suggesting that the ocean view will provide them an opportunity to watch dolphins at play; four bedrooms means a bedroom for each child and even a maid's room; skylights throughout for a light, airy atmosphere; and extra garage space for a tool bench.

Color your sales presentation with interesting anecdotes and word pictures that help your potential customers put themselves in the picture of using your product or service.

At a greenhouse nearby, my favorite gardener tells the story of the couple who bought a plant for their herb garden one day and came back the next day for three more, explaining that they had eaten the whole plant in the salad the night before. I imagine that he tells that story every time someone comes to buy fresh herb plants. And every time it sells a new customer on cinnamon basil!

To sell a gourmet cook on trading a beach house for her farmhouse in Tuscany one summer, she was tempted her with a true story. Cinnamon and sweet basil and other fresh herbs such as curly parsley, thyme, lots of rosemary, and even chocolate mint had been planted in the window boxes in her honor. Then she was asked for other special requests. Who could resist?

Instead of badgering prospects with what you have to sell, entice them with something they need and will want to buy. And make sure you really know why people buy what you are selling. Stock brokers don't sell stocks, they sell financial security. Doctors don't sell medicine, they sell the promise of good health. Ready for Media doesn't sell communications training, it sells confidence in communication.

Easy Does It

One of my favorite T-shirt slogans exclaims that life is short, eat dessert first. But another school of sales recommends saving the presentation dessert for last, until after you have interest, qualified the budget, and gotten the decision. Too many times a waiter's recitation of all the specials confuses the poor patrons and leads to a lot of repeating.

In Hollywood, waiting tables is the day job of many actors and actresses who are hip to the practice of reflecting the question, "What do you suggest? with "What do you like?" So, begin the interest phase with leading questions to let the prospect paint a picture of the needs and desires that match your product and service. We do this with leading questions such as: Which of your executives will be spokespeople? Do you have a public relations firm to get coverage for you once we help you refine and know how to deliver your messages? What media are you interested in appearing on and in?

Not until the presentation phase will we tell him that Ready for Media has coached corporate executives, celebrities, and sports stars for interviews on the *Today Show*, *60 Minutes*, *Nightline*, *QVC*, *PC Week*, *BusinessWeek*, *The Wall Street Journal*, *Time Magazine*, *Fortune*, *People Magazine*, and numerous infomercials, Webcasts and satellite media tours.

During this creation phase, listen for details in her scenario that you don't provide, and deal with them gently but firmly to determine her qualifications as a buyer for your goods or services. If it's not on the menu and you can't find a suitable substitute, they won't be having dinner in your establishment.

And what menu comes without prices?

So, find out the budget, in round numbers. I usually ask, "Are we talking thousands or tens of thousands?" Sometimes, I simply tell the prospect that our services include...and typically range in price from...and ask if it is in his budget. If not, and they have already created a word picture of exactly what they want, next year's budget is probably already in the works.

Too many clients have heard that, "the first person to mention the price, loses," so they often won't tell you what investment they are willing to make. A good friend of mine calls her wardrobe consultation "investment dressing," implying that every piece in the wardrobe is a contribution to the whole of being well dressed. I do the same.

I once had a Fortune 500 company executive tell me, "I have exactly $1,000 to spend." It wasn't much, but his candor saved us time and was so refreshing that it bought him the two hours he needed because we wanted his company on our client list.

The Decision-Maker

Far too often, we spend time saying all the right things to the wrong people. And nobody wants to admit that they don't have that power or authority. One of the best ways to weed out the influencer is to meet him or her in person. When you are making a new business pitch or introducing a product, see who the audience looks to as the opinion leader. It happened for us in Tokyo when the general manager took a liking to media coaching and his lieutenants were not far behind. When you successfully engage the opinion leader, you've probably engaged the group.

On the Phone

28

*Well, if I called the wrong number, why did you
answer the phone?*

—James Thurber

It is thought by some that the explosion in portable phone
popularity simply proves that most of us are unwilling to live
without someone else's agreement every 10 minutes or so.

And while manufacturers once discovered value in practi-
cally giving you the razor so you would buy the blades, now we
are pretty much given the phone, we just have to pay for the
privilege to use it, month after month. Yet the latest and greatest in wireless technology, with more minutes than some of us
can use in a lifetime, doesn't come with directions on what to
say and how to say it.

Outgoing Phone Messages

An increasing number of my friends and business associates record detailed directions to their callers on how to leave a voice-mail message. "Please say your name and phone number slowly and clearly at the beginning of your message..." begins one. Another suggests, "Please say your phone number clearly, even if you think I have it, so I can call you back more quickly."

Recording a new outgoing message each morning with the day's date to give callers a roadmap to your day and the likelihood, or lack thereof, that they will hear back from you is also becoming popular.

Incoming Phone Messages

How often have you gotten a phone message that was recorded so quickly that no amount of replay could make it decipherable? Or one that rambled for the full two minutes before your machine cut the person off, without the phone number? Speaking slowly, carefully, and concisely is vitally important to the impression you leave with your message. You don't want to be the caller who clearly doesn't have enough to do but stay on the phone!

Phone technology gives a decided advantage to voices in the lower ranges and therefore, most often, to men. As a businesswoman, particularly when leaving messages on answering machines from a cell that may be also be retrieved from location, I've had to learn to speak as low and slow as I can.

Surprisingly, in many cases, a $13 landline will leave a clearer message than the most expensive cell phone. If you have a choice in leaving a message, choose the wired wonder. And know ahead of time what items to include in your message and the order in which you want to deliver them. You will distinguish yourself and be appreciated for not wasting others' time if you keep your messages within 15 to 30 seconds. Deliver it with a smile on your face, which can be heard in your voice.

Cell Phones

In 1997, Olli Kallasvuo, an executive at Nokia came to Los Angeles from Finland for media coaching and cultural tips for his upcoming Asian tour.

"One day," he said, "you won't have to 'find a phone.' The phone will come everywhere with you and everyone will have his or her own." Who knew it would come to this? Mr. Kallasvuo did.

Now many of us around the world have become like kids with a new toy. But as movie and TV ads often recommend, "discretion advised."

Because the technology is so new, mobile manners are still evolving. But the conventional wisdom is that it is just plain rude to interrupt one in-person conversation to begin another, on the phone. At best, be selective in who has your cell phone number and confident in your phone's message-taking capability to allow you to return the call at your earliest convenience. At the very least, ask permission of the person who is with you if you may just answer and return the call later. If the call is very important and/or extremely time sensitive, ask to be excused and take the call as quickly as possible away from others. Without the benefit of phone booths or soundproofed cubicles, phone calls are often very loud and interruptive.

Meetings, restaurants, golf courses, tennis courts, libraries, health clubs, spas, and many other places have banned the mobile monsters because of their distracting nature. On airplanes and in hospitals, they must be turned off to avoid disrupting sensitive equipment. And in some cities, handheld phones are outlawed while driving. All for good reason.

Conference Calls

A very cost-effective feature on multi-line phones is conference calling, where you can include several callers in one conversation with the push of a button. It's often the answer to scheduling conflicts, a "he said," "she said," situation or one in which you need consensus. When there are several people in the room and a speakerphone is used, participants should identify themselves before speaking, taking care not to talk over each other.

Quarterly Reports

SEC Regulation FD has changed the rules about communicating with investors, analysts, and the media. It has also magnified the importance of the quarterly conference call (which was routinely referred to as the quarterly *earnings* report until the technology bubble burst). It used to be that a CEO could correct a mistake or mis-impression with an analyst or reporter privately. Now, corporate governance makes that impossible. Selective disclosure is illegal.

According to one corporate director of investor relations, "Web casting has exploded the significance of the quarterly financial results by a factor of 10 times." Not only do industry analysts and both financial and business media interview your CEO and CFO online, John and Jane Q. Stockholder and their brokers are listening in as well.

The stock price rises and falls because of a one-on-one conversation between the key executives and dozens to hundreds of listeners, hearing it live or on tape. "Did you make your numbers?" "What is your guidance going forward?" Public companies won't get another chance to make a good impression until next quarter—or maybe never.

Circulating a constant stream of press releases to an ever-widening circle and creating online conference calls with analysts and reporters is a nemesis for publicly traded companies these days. Once again, Marshall McLuhan proves to be prophetic. The medium is a powerful message in providing a window into the world of the corporate suite.

What should the chief officers say? And how should they say it? Does the CEO provide some color to the CFO's play by play. Does the CFO agree with the CEO's vision of the company, and how well will they work together to get there?

This sometimes hour-long shot is posted on the company's Website until it's replaced by the next one to be heard 24/7 by anyone with access to the Internet.

Every three months, some companies put a great deal of time and money into scripting and practicing for these events, with mock questions for the participants. Others don't. All too often, the powers-that-be delude themselves into thinking that this is "just another phone call." And a low stock price reflects it.

Just as public relations and human resources use outside consultants to test their programs and their people, investor relations should do the same when it comes to a litmus test for the stock's spokespeople. This is not the time you want to begin preaching to the choir, and it's a rare choirboy who risks his position by daring to properly confront God's chosen ones.

Like any media coverage, a quarterly conference call is a key opportunity for a company to tell its story. The people who are charged as spokespeople for the company are also challenged to make sure their stories are well represented. Being prepared *before* the conference call is the only solution in feeling comfortable speaking to all those stakeholders. Every practice session should include:

- Producing the call by preparing and editing the commentary to be heard.
- Practicing spokespeople to be concise, conversational, and confident when reporting.

- Putting the company's results in an industry perspective.

- Offering audio feedback and constructive critique.

- Coaching the spokespeople to put emphasis on the company's vision of the future (Wall Street doesn't care as much about where you've been as where you're going).

- Helping to reflect corporate branding, written and presented in a way that is consistent with the rest of the communications messages.

- Challenging the CEO and CFO with both questions that they're concerned about and ones they haven't even thought of yet.

In short, you should design and deliver a quarterly report that works for, not *against*, you.

Rallying the Troops

You can't think and hit at the same time.

—Yogi Berra

One of the most quoted and beloved baseball managers of all time went on to say, "if you ask me, this is true with any sport. I said it in 1946 when I was with the Newark Bears playing Triple A ball. My manager told me not to swing at balls out of the strike zone. He said, 'Yogi, next time you're up, think about what you're doing.' I struck out in three pitches."

Up to Bat

When speaking to audiences of your peers and reports, what you have to say should be second nature when you get up to bat. It's what you know and what you do all the time.

One Little League baseball coach whose day job is managing a division at a giant aerospace company had to address his direct reports on a change in direction. The human resources director who hired Ready for Media to coach this division head explained that the executive was in too high a position to just "talk to the slides." She directed us to coach him in sharing the company's vision with a sense of fun and passion.

In exploring the executive's interests, hobbies, and passions, we learned that Yogi Berra was one of his all-time heroes. He, like many, loves this baseball legend for the plain wisdom of his one-of-a-kind observations. Yogisms are a different language. Funny. Profound. Poignant.

Sports are so analogous to business and for most of us, games we like to watch or pick up on weekends. So, choose your favorite sport and you will find wisdom in it for your own team.

UCLA's winningest basketball coach, John Wooden, motivated his championship teams with, "Be quick but don't hurry." And football great Vince Lombardi said in a 1962 interview that "winning isn't everything but wanting to win is." This was homogenized into the reported battle cry for rallying the troops, "Winning isn't everything, it's the only thing."

Our aerospace manager used Yogi's pronouncement that "the future ain't what it used to be" in one address to new hires. "When you come to a fork in the road, take it" became the theme for a briefing to design engineers. And he quoted the time when Yogi was asked what time it is, Yogi asked, "You mean now?" in a speech titled, "The Time Is Now."

This aerospace guru told me in a follow-up call that he uses Yogisms in his everyday leadership practice as well, "Once when Yogi was asked, 'What makes a good manager?' he said, 'Good players.'"

With a little coaching, our manager (also known as "Coach" to his Little Leaguers) found a similar and unique role in the workplace. Now he is as legendary on his professional playing field for always citing the appropriate wisdom of a Yogism.

Batting Practice

An exercise I often do with clients is to first ask them to stand up and record on tape two minutes about their job or some aspect of it. Then, without sitting down, to do another two minutes on their favorite subject. The subjects vary from their kids to golf to boating to volunteer work to a stamp collection. The list is endless. But the reaction is always the same. Almost without exception, when speaking about the job where they spend the majority of their waking hours, they are wooden, monotone and uninspiring. When they get to passions, they become animated with gestures, eye contact, and a lively, conversational tone. Suddenly, the mission seems to be convincingly clear: to share the music of their lives.

Picasso said, "To draw is to close your eyes and dance." What music are you dancing to? Your job, as a communicator, is merely to transfer the passion and music of your life into the expression of your work or project or subject. It is, after all, your life's work, your contribution to society. Your job, since you've chosen to accept it, probably holds within it your leadership potential and possibility.

As communications coaches, my team and I are merely holding up a mirror to reflect your expressions. By helping you find passion once again for the work you do and express it, your business briefings and speeches will become much more exciting and inspirational. Bottom line, don't seek to inform, seek to motivate and inspire.

Find the Time

An entertainment executive was so jammed at work that he had gotten into a bad habit of keeping his staff waiting until the last minute to write his speeches, nevermind practicing. With only hours until the event, panic prevailed until he walked on stage and read his staff's much too detailed, nuts and bolts account of the new season, without sharing the vision or passion that was making them the leading network. Everyone was disappointed, not the least of which was he.

Finally, his staff coerced him into finding three hours on each of several Sunday afternoons at his house to let us work. His staff attended as well. The prospect of his sharing the vision that made him a great leader was worth missing a pro football game or two. Their willingness to give up weekend time impressed him not only with their dedication but that he may have something important to say, after all.

Weeks in advance, we began facilitating the communication between the executive and his staff of: Who the audience is, why this is important to them, what they need and want to know from him and his vision, and how he will get their attention. Once this TV mogul grasped the economies of scale that a focused and passionate 20-minute presentation followed by Q&A could ignite the imaginations of hundreds in his audience, he finds the time, every time.

The Medium Is the Message

There's an old saying in the newspaper trade that good news is no news. But Shakespeare more accurately reflected the reality of corporate suites, "Though it be honest, it is never good to bring bad news." Still, news is a fact of business life, and when you must deliver it, choosing the delivery system is as important as crafting what you will say.

The new president of a giant insurance company made that mistake when he sent a cold and stiff "talking head" videotape of himself to the 10,000 employees in the worldwide branches of his company. Every screening room was silent after the CEO's announcement that his restructuring plans would include more or less significant layoffs. There was little the regional managers could do or say after that bomb was dropped.

A perhaps much more appropriate communications tool was the live 25-city interactive, satellite media tour one of our clients used in a similar situation. Our CEO explained compassionately that he would have preferred being with each group in person but that in order to reach all his employees simultaneously with this difficult news, he had chosen this venue. The manager at each location proctored live audience questions for the CEO about the restructuring until every one was answered over the following two hours.

If you do decide to have an interactive, multi-city satellite tour, make sure that every detail is checked and rechecked. Never is it more true that you only get one chance to make a good first impression than on a live satellite broadcast.

We once reported to the *Wall Street Journal* the true story of one CEO, not wanting to mar the front of his $200 tie, who pinned the lavaliere microphone the technician had handed him on the back of the tie. For the first three minutes of his announcement, his lips moved but no sound was heard. He began again after a behind-the-scenes executive decision was made for a technician to reach into the shot and re-position the microphone to the outside of his lapel. To this day, the CEO hasn't lived it down.

E-Mail Etiquette

The better part of valor is discretion.
—William Shakespeare

Shakespeare's words ring true certainly nowhere as much as on e-mail.

Sitting next to a human resources director on a plane, I shared the dream of writing this book. She said if I did, she would buy a copy for every one of the 4,000 people in her company. "Every day," she bemoaned, "our employees prove themselves to be inarticulate, hot-headed, and ignorant when it comes to sending e-mails and presenting themselves and our products both internally and externally." I've kept her card.

And it's not just the ignorant ones among us. A recently graduated lawyer in a summer program being paid more than $10,000 a month at New York's top law firm bragged to a friend by e-mail. "[I'm] busy doing 'jack sh*t,' going to 2-hour lunches, typing [personal] e-mails and bullsh*tting with people while appearing not to be a 'f#ckup.'" His arrogance was exceeded only by his ignorance in mistakenly circulating it, not to his friend, but throughout the firm, including to at least 40 partners.

The story was related to me by the partner of another firm, in another city. The *summer's* e-mail was published verbatim in *The New Yorker*, which chided him for inadvertently following the *New York Law Journal*'s advice for the summer's associate class ("Stand Out in a Crowd.... You still have to distinguish yourself from lots of other very bright people").

This is the kind of watershed moment that leads to the classic reprimands "you'll never work in this town again" and "it will take a long time to live that one down." Or in the understatement of his written apology, "I recognize the damage done to my firm-wide reputation and possibly to my future."

When a young lawyer who's been all the way through the most prestigious undergraduate and law schools in the country doesn't realize that an e-mail is a written document with all of the legalities and proprieties expected therein, what hope is there for the rest of us? Except perhaps to learn from his mistake.

Except that he had obviously not learned from those who had gone before him. Two years earlier, an intern's exit e-mail whined about another company's bigotry towards his Italian-American heritage and his obviously superior behavior in not joining his fellow interns in getting "sh*t-faced" drunk or blatantly using cocaine in people's offices. That same year, a 24-year-old employee from another prestigious school was working abroad. He alerted about a dozen friends back home by e-mail of his lavish and decadent lifestyle on company time and money. His enthusiasm quickly spread across several continents, and back across his boss's desk. He doesn't work there anymore.

Power Tools

So now you know what not to write, but how do you actually take advantage of electronic mail, the greatest communication tool ever invented? Let's start with some practical stuff.

Business e-mail should be written less like a letter and more like a newspaper lead. Every good journalist knows that the headline (your subject line) must say it all and the first paragraph should give the five *W*s and an *H*: Who, What, When, Where, Why, and How. Additional paragraphs may give more details, but be sure they are needed.

And nothing is more frustrating than to compose the perfect correspondence only to have your computer freeze and have to begin all over again. The save draft feature allows you to save the draft as you work on the great American e-mail.

Many Internet programs have basic spell check, numbering, and bullet points. Also, keep Microsoft Office open while you are e-mailing, not only to check spelling and grammar, but also for the thesaurus in the tools box/language on the menu bar. Finding the right word to express your thought not only makes you a more articulate communicator but increases your vocabulary at the same time. Plus, it tells you whether your use of the word is a noun, adjective, verb, or adverb so you'll know if you are using it correctly as well.

Documents, formal letters, and anything else that depends on layout are best created on a Word page and then attached. This also allows you to center copy and use flush left and right margins. Before attaching, save the document under an easy-to-find name or place without using numbers or symbols and concluding with .doc. This enhances the likelihood that your recipient will be able to open the attachment, especially if you are bridging a Mac and a PC. Choose formats that are as common as possible to further ensure that the attachment can be opened easily. Because attachments require being saved to someone's computer before opening and take up great space if they include pictures, sound, etc., use them with discretion. Sometimes, a one-page document can just be cut and pasted onto the end of your e-mail to increase the likelihood that it will be read!

For a writer of e-mails, the best features of all are cut, copy, and paste in the edit box on the menu bar. Whole sentences and paragraphs can be moved on a document by cutting and pasting. Copy can be used to repeat a list or phrase or paragraph from almost anywhere by just highlighting (dragging the pointer over the original), copying, and pasting. You are limited only by your own imagination, and copyright laws!

And spell check, spell check, spell check! Again on Microsoft Office, correct the spelling as soon as you see the red line under the word that is misspelled. The green line for grammar is a little more baffling but can be the first clue that you've made a grammatical error, have too many spaces, a rambling or run-on sentence, and so on.

But even spell check misses words that are spelled correctly but misused and proper nouns such as names. On a recent bill I received for property insurance, the agent had misspelled his own street address. Even though he had conducted himself very professionally throughout our first year of doing business together, I grew suddenly wary that his poor attention to detail would jeopardize his handling of a damage claim. Much to his chagrin and deep regret, I changed insurance agents and companies. The devil, as they say, is in the details.

Make sure that your e-mail is correctly addressed and that, if it's important, you request a return receipt to know if and when it was opened by your addressee. Carbon copies (CC) show the recipient everyone who was copied on the correspondence and blind carbon copy (BCC), is so called because your recipient won't see who received the copy. Use BCC: very sparingly and only for good reason because people prefer to know who else is witnessing correspondence e-mailed to them.

The CC feature can put pressure on someone to do something they've agreed to do, prove that you are doing what you've agreed to do, or at least keep all interested or relevant parties informed and in the loop. Carbon copying will avoid the retort, "Why didn't you tell me about this?" or help defray the excuse, "I didn't know about it so, of course, I never followed through."

Your "Sent" box will serve as a record of everything sent by you on e-mail. If it was sent to an incorrect address, it should return to you as "unable to deliver."

If you are an e-mail packrat, watch out! Even the www (World Wide Web), or at least your window on it, has limited space. Electronically file or commit to paper the most important e-mails and trash the rest. A cluttered Inbox, not unlike your desk, may be the sign of a creative but cluttered mind.

And finally, timing. Is there a statute of limitations on e-mail? How long can you wait to respond? Is it ever too late to return an e-mail and how long should you wait for a reply before trying again?

It all depends on the subject and your relationship to the addressee. It's best to answer an e-mail as soon as possible but sometimes a few days is acceptable. If you don't have or know the answer yet, acknowledging receipt and giving an approximate timeline is usually appreciated. Typically, people send e-mail with the expectation of an answer.

As a general rule, e-mails are not missed. They get right through and touch the recipient in an up close and personal way. So, correspondent, beware...and be careful of what you send.

Rights and Responsibilities

Corporate America has never opened a Pandora's box like the Internet. Executives and employees alike are more or less on the honor system to be working not playing (creating and sending personal e-mails, forwarding jokes, playing videogames, watching movies) on the information highway during business hours.

In many companies today, there are not only firewalls, but e-mail police who do random checks on each employee's e-mail. At one very large brokerage firm, the rule is for employees to immediately trash inappropriate e-mail and politely inform whoever sent it that it is not acceptable at their company. Further, these financial consultants are not allowed to e-mail clients from home computers because it jeopardizes clients' confidential files.

My own employees contributed these suggestions:

1. Don't send personal e-mail from work! It's unprofessional and unpredictable. You never know who might be watching and telling.

2. Have a business e-mail and a personal one. Keep them separate.

3. Don't send a personal e-mail to someone else at work, unless it is absolutely necessary.

4. Don't put your business e-mail on any mailing lists. Mailing lists get sold to others with whom you most likely don't want to be associated. There is nothing more embarrassing than for your boss to walk in and see porn on your computer screen.

5. Be wary of mail from someone you don't know, and never click on any suspicious links in an e-mail. You never know what site or virus could be lurking there.

6. When you receive an e-mail that seems too good to be true, it probably is. If you've entered a contest, perhaps you've won, but most likely, you've won a virus.

Ready, Fire, Aim

Nowhere is the KISS (Keep It Short & Simple, Sweetheart) principle as important as in e-mail. E-mails that can be read at a glance are everyone's favorite.

And "paper" is cheap, so send just one subject per e-page. But time is not, so respect both your own and your audience's time by making your point simply and clearly.

Your style should be casual but correct. For example, it sounds stilted to write, "With whom are you coming to the meeting?" But there's no reason to use poor English and dangle your participles either by choosing to write, "Who are you coming with?" "Who's coming with you?" would be better.

Proper nouns versus pronouns usually lead to less confusion. Use "Jon" instead of "he" or "him"; "our new software program, The Basics in a Box" instead of "it"; and "my interns Kim and Gabe," instead of "they."

Despite its efficiency in time and money, an e-mail is a one-way street that doesn't give the feedback to tell if we're going in the right direction. You can't read their faces or adjust the tone of your voice. It's a high-speed highway with no turning back. And words always seem more important when they are written than spoken.

Whenever time allows, stash your important correspondence in the draft file, even for an hour. Then read it again when its "cold" to see how it sounds and feels. This Ready, Fire, Aim technique allows you to sit at your recipient's desk and experience receiving your words.

Is it too cold (abrupt), pushy (starting sentences with action words), nasty (full of sarcasm), or overly familiar and gushy (solicitous but insincere)? Do you ramble instead of getting to the point? Most importantly, could your words easily be misread in a different voice to take on a different flavor (for example, sarcasm and criticism) and mean something else?

Make the necessary changes and "send now" with greater confidence.

Show respect for e-mail. Because of its convenience, immediacy and cost-effectiveness, e-mail has become ubiquitous in business. In many instances, it alone represents and speaks for you. Use it with discretion.

Meetings

There is more to this than meets the eye.

—Anonymous

"He's in a meeting" is either a very good excuse for not taking calls or most businesspeople do spend their entire work lives in meetings. I suspect a little of both.

In fact, it's estimated that out of an average eight-hour day, two to five hours of a mid-level manager's time is devoted entirely to meetings. Research shows that among top executives, a whopping six and a half hours of every eight is devoted solely to meetings.

Bad enough if they were judged to be profitable, but surveyed professionals indicate that more than half the time spent in meetings is wasted. "We just meet and meet and meet and never seem to do anything," complained the senior manager of network operations at Federal Express with exasperation in an article for *Fast Company* titled "The Seven Sins of Deadly Meetings." Further, 46 percent of respondents in an MCI White Paper survey reported they attend more meetings today than they did one year ago.

Equate that to dollars and lost time by otherwise productive employees, whose own work usually suffers from lack of attention or requires overtime. Companies are losing big bucks to meetings, an estimated $37 billion dollars according to the U.S. Bureau of Labor Statistics. And with no individual accountability, whatever progress is made in meetings is often not managed effectively anyway.

The next time you are bored in a meeting, do the math by adding up the hourly pay of who's there. And it's not just the hours spent *in* the meeting, but also those spent *on* the meeting. It is estimated that a one-hour meeting of four people will probably take another 16 hours of salaried, support time. The indirect costs of a failed meeting in terms of loss of momentum, motivation, clarity, direction, delegation, persuasion, time, leadership, accomplishment, teamwork, and reputations is incalculable.

George David Kieffer, a partner in the national law firm of Manatt Phelps & Phillips in Los Angeles and author of the book *The Strategy of Meetings* interviewed more than 50 of America's most successful and respected leaders in business, labor, industry, education, and government—many of whom are viewed as masters in the art of conducting meetings. Two central points emerged from his interviews. Number one, most professionals do not recognize the enormous impact their meetings have on their organizations and the resulting corporate cultures. And two, according to Kieffer and his band of renowned experts, the skill to manage a meeting—to develop ideas, to motivate people, and to move people and ideas to positive action—is perhaps the most critical asset in any career.

Before we get to making rather than breaking your career over meetings, let's focus on why meetings matter to your corporate culture. In a business world that is faster, meaner, and more downsized than ever before, there should be more individual initiative, more e-mails, and fewer meetings, right? Wrong. Apparently, more and more companies with fewer and fewer people are increasingly depending on more and more meetings for team-based decision-making. And, obviously, bad meetings that waste everyone's time, talent, and sense of accomplishment create a source of negative energy about our companies and ourselves.

Good meeting protocol should not be proprietary information. Everyone should know and practice it. Teaching everyone in your organization the skills of good meetings is somewhat like the savvy marketing move made by the authors of *The One Minute Manager*, Dr. Spencer Johnson and Ken Blanchard.

"Give everyone to whom you report and who reports to you, a copy of the book," they advised. Not only did this advice sell a lot of books, it made One-Minute Management a good business practice embraced at all levels.

In the *Fast Company* article, author Eric Matson wrote that most people sin by not taking meetings seriously. "They arrive late, leave early and spend most of their time doodling, then follow the mantra that the meeting is over, let's get back to work."

What should you ask to know if the meeting in question is necessary?

1.   What is the goal or what do we want to accomplish. In other words, a win from this meeting would be...?
2.   Is it the right time and right atmosphere? Are all the facts, the right leader, and needed participants available?

3. Could this be accomplished as well in a phone conversation between two or a conference call among three?

4. Do we have more immediate deadlines?

So, why don't mindless meetings stop? The reasons are as endless and boring as the meetings themselves. But basically, according to Kieffer, it's Newton's First Law: The Law of Inertia. Every object persists in its state of rest, or uniform motion; unless, it is compelled to change that state, by forces impressed upon it.

Similarly, meetings go on and on forever and in the same manner unless you act upon them with an equal or greater force.

You could "Just say, 'No.'" In *No Longer Human*, Japanese novelist Dazai Osamu wrote, "My unhappiness was the unhappiness of a person who could not say no." Eleanor Roosevelt said "no one can make you feel inferior without your consent." Likewise, no one can make a meeting without people who are willing to meet. In a 1966 article for *McCall's* magazine, Charlotte Keyes titled her words, "Suppose They Gave a War, and No One Came."

Before we discuss a passive-aggressive approach of what meetings to attend or conduct, we must explore what objectives are best accomplished by a meeting.

Successful Meeting Objectives

Brainstorming

Meetings devoted exclusively to brainstorming are a great way to tap the creative energy of a group. Hollywood producer Ken Atchity describes the process of vision to revision by stressing how important it is to let your right brain write before your left brain edits. The same is true in a brainstorming meeting. Every idea should be encouraged because it may lead to the idea or solution you need. Only after the right brains have created with joyous abandon should the left brains weed through for the "right" answer.

It is interesting to note that since predominately male-oriented meetings are a linear affair, where b follows a, etc., if your process is a more creative or circular approach, wait to interject your solution until the meeting is ready for it.

A Vote

When a decision calls for a democratic rather than autocratic conclusion, a meeting can be a means to that end. To satisfy everyone's desire to make an informed decision, it's important that all the participants have all the necessary information ahead of time. The information-gathering, the lobbying, and the personal decision-making should be done before everyone gets there.

If the boss has convened a meeting to share a decision that has already been reached, don't be the staff member who persists in debating it. You're in the wrong meeting and not impressing anyone!

As a general rule, subordinates should be gathering information. Superiors should be creating policy.

Delegation

"Who's on first?" was a tireless joke between Abbott and Costello. It also speaks to the challenge of a committee chair not knowing what he or she wants. And therefore, one who cannot delegate effectively or even lead a meeting in which the group as a whole delegates assignments. Before leaving a delegating meeting, be sure to ask what is expected of you and when.

Inspiration

Even though every meeting must inspire the group to commit to the objective, some meetings are all about inspiration.

The two greatest mistakes made in meetings are not knowing what you want to accomplish and trying to accomplish everything at once.

But what do you do if your boss or her boss is an overmeeter? The best advice is to offer your boss the choice of having you finish a more pressing assignment rather than attend this meeting. Focusing the boss on priorities may get everyone off an unnecessary hook. Even she probably knows management expert Peter Drucker's warning that we either work or we meet, we can't do both at the same time.

The meeting is only a means to an end. As the quarterback in your job, career, and meeting, the boss calls the plays. He brings everyone together with a specific plan. Once that's accomplished, the play begins. But until everyone gets out of the huddle, there is no game!

Just as in the football huddle, no extraneous players should be allowed. You don't empty the bench just so everyone can feel included. Be more selective about your meeting partners, then give everyone you need everything they need to execute the play.

The 8-P Approach

The **Point**. Before you define the purpose, ask yourself or whoever is calling you away from your life's work, "What's the point?" Even before you define the purpose, you have to consider whether there's a worthwhile point to having a meeting.

The **Purpose**. What key objective needs to be accomplished? The fewer the objectives, the more likely that they will be accomplished.

The **Power**. Who is quarterbacking this meeting? What do you need from your players?

The **People**. For many years my parents gave the best parties around. When asked the one secret of their success, they always say, "The people make the party." That's true, but I always suspect that it is also their way of complimenting their guests by making them feel important and worthy of being there. It certainly wasn't empty praise. Their people were the best guests. There was no "B" list. Outgoing, ingratiating guests who came to have a good time and make it a good time for everyone else as well. In short, they contributed.

The **Plan**. If you've ever done a new business proposal, you know that it's all done on paper first. When you finally win the business, all that's left is executing. That's why many companies charge for the proposal because that's where the creative work happens. In theory, the client could shop your proposal and hand the plan to anyone for any price. The only thing that needs to be accomplished in the presentation is buy off or agreement.

The quality time you spend deciding what you want your meeting to accomplish and sharing the goal with your attendees will greatly affect how the meeting plays. As a **player**, don't run with the ball until your quarterback spells out where you are to go.

The **Promotion**. How are you going to sell your meeting? Figure out what's in it for each of the team members and tell them, before expecting them to show up.

The **Progress**. At the end of every workshop, we ask each participant to fill out a questionnaire on what was accomplished in getting Ready for Media. "What was the most valuable thing you learned in the coaching? What was the least?" In short, what they've heard is much more important than what we've said.

In many sports, there is only a win or a loss, never a tie. It's not by accident that they call it sudden death. I once had a meeting that felt more like a near-death experience. It was with one of the hottest producers in Hollywood to whom I'd been recommended as a speech writer and coach. After we'd worked together for awhile, he asked his secretary to make a luncheon meeting with me at his favorite restaurant. What I failed to learn until later, when I finally pieced it together, was that he regularly lunched with people whom he thought could teach him something about their worlds. Not realizing the purpose of the meeting and being much more familiar with the role of interviewer than interviewed, I totally disappointed him. Finally, after acting like a doe in headlights trying to talk about myself, I pitched him the movie I was writing at the time. He offered a few ideas, but overall, the meeting was a failure, and I didn't get any more chances to write for him either.

Without knowing his agenda, by querying his secretary or the public relations executive who originally recommended me and without having an agenda of my own except to show up, I failed us both.

The **Payoff**. How do you judge a meeting? Was the group and cause worthy of the participants' time? Did each have an opportunity to influence the outcome?

A Powerful meeting is one in which the whole is greater than the sum of the parts. There should be a synergistic effect of bringing those people together with that plan for that purpose. It's not enough for a meeting to just keep the participants informed. There's e-mail for that. It is estimated that our ability to comprehend what we read is three to four times greater than our ability to comprehend what we are told.

After a meeting, ask yourself what more, better, or different happened as a result. Before the next one, ask yourself the same question. Specifically, what has been or still needs to be accomplished?

Following the business principle of spending money before you make it, spending time that you don't have to plan meetings you don't want to go to may seem somewhat counterproductive. With fewer employees in the workforce, many feel there's hardly enough time in a day to complete basic tasks. Who has the time or energy to plan meetings so strenuously? Was or will it be a win or a loss? How do you know? Why should you care? Remember Kieffer's belief that the skill to manage a meeting is the most critical asset in any career.

Not a Dirty Word

Control. Another "C" word. Charles de Gaulle was of the belief that men (and presumably women, too) can no more get along without direction than they can without eating, drinking, and sleeping. And George David Kieffer is of the opinion that you will achieve the goals of benefiting yourself and your career, your cause and your company to the extent that you are willing and able to exert positive control over every meeting you attend.

First, declining a meeting until conditions are favorable: the homework is done, the environment and timing seem ideal, and the necessary people are available is both your right and your responsibility.

Before you can reject or accept a meeting, you need to consider the smokescreens that meetings provide: a substitute for work, commiserating, networking, grandstanding, or gossiping. Remember, meetings multiply.

Power vs. Productivity

Routine meetings are the power monger's playground. He or she can boss people around, control their time, and reinforce the pecking order. If, on the other hand, you seek to be productive, eliminate regularly scheduled meetings.

As a manager, I was once told by a Harvard MBA, "Get good people, then get out of the way."

To be successful, "calling it in" killing time in a meeting, drifting to and through them, is not good enough. You must demand from others and contribute more yourself.

Has experience proven that no matter what you are trying
to do, it usually gets down to a meeting? Consider the alternative that technology makes possible: an e-mail with copies to all
concerned.

How do you know when to write, phone, or meet? Written
communication takes time, but people do pay attention and concisely written e-mails are read. Talking it out seems easier, but
talking can be a greater time-waster, unless you know whom to
talk to and what to say.

Eulogies

...till death do us part.

—the Book of Common Prayer

Depending on the circumstances of a death and the religion, memorial services are becoming more popular than funerals. Increasingly, they are thought of as a celebration of the person's life instead of a cause for mourning.

If you are orchestrating such an event, it is important to tell the attendees how to participate and exactly what you want them to do. Walk through in your mind exactly what friends need to know, right down to the directions to a church, gravesite, or home. A friend of mine admitted that he once arrived at the wrong funeral because he confused churches and he wasn't given an address!

What are the expectations in a Jewish home when you sit Shiva? Are visitors allowed or expected to take communion at a Catholic Church? What is expected of attendees in a Muslim or Buddhist ceremony? People want to be respectful at a time like this, but you have to tell them how.

In creating your own service, according to one clergywoman I interviewed, there should be three main parts. Firstly, thanks and praise for the life should be given. Secondly, the friends and extended family should share their personal feelings and experiences. Thirdly, attendees want to be reminded that as life goes on, the departed will always be remembered and live on in the hearts of all gathered there.

If you are called upon by the family to give part of the service, make sure that you can do it without completely breaking down. A few tears or becoming slightly choked up does happen when the feelings are sincere, but becoming completely overwhelmed with the sadness of the moment and having to be led away does not serve the occasion. You will be forgiven more readily for not speaking than for being less than dignified when you do. If you suddenly find yourself too overwhelmed to go on, don't.

In the past, the immediate family was sequestered to mourn privately, but as customs become more casual, family members are beginning to take a more active role in the eulogy. A thoughtful clergyman came to the aid of a 13-year-old daughter who had overestimated her command of emotions by simply coming to stand at her side for support. His mere presence gave her the added strength she needed to finish the words that were so important to her to impart. Another clergywoman always asks the family for a signal or code that means "I can't go on, please rescue or finish for me." Giving your clergy person this permission ahead of time can ensure that things will run more smoothly.

Very often, various people will be asked to represent and speak to different time periods (the early years or mid life) or the different aspects (business, sports, community involvement) of a person's life.

Most any clergy person will tell you that one of the biggest challenges is coming up to speed on the details of a life at the very last minute. The media, of course, has a tribute to every famous person over the age of 60 in the planning stages so they will not be caught off guard without the best clips when the time comes.

If you are going to acknowledge family members or other mourners, make sure you know exactly how to pronounce their names. The audience probably knows these people better than you do and will be somewhat unforgiving if you don't get it right. How well you didn't know the person is not a very good approach either.

Sometimes, anyone who wishes to speak is invited to do so. To avoid rambling, have a mental outline of what you want to include. True-life stories that put the deceased in a good light or ones that share the humor of situations you experienced with him or her are your best bet. It probably goes without saying that no one in your audience will appreciate anything that could be construed as critical or mean-spirited. Backstabbing would be redundant since your victim is already dead. If all is fair in love and war, then all must be forgiven in death.

Preparation

As with any other presentation, you should take as much time as possible ahead of the actual service to prepare. Share some of the funny and endearing moments you or others experienced with the deceased. Pick funny or poignant real-life stories that are not embarrassing to anyone but that typify the person's beloved idiosyncrasies and uniqueness. Experiences that begin with the phrase, "I'll never forget the time that" or "The funniest thing that ever happened to us was" are usually good openers. Sometimes little known facts such as where a nickname came from or a prophetic childhood experience will bond the group and make everyone feel a little closer. Include the things that made you and everyone else love the departed.

Tell of your experiences as a comedian would, very concisely and with a punch line. In other words, know where you are going and stop the minute you get there. Perhaps string three or four one-minute stories together from your happy memories and those of others close to him or her. Begin with the second best and save the very best for last, but get to it quickly so the audience is still interested in your payoff.

Or use the stories to punctuate the history of the person or your period in her life or his. And still have a good close. Appropriate passages from the Old or New Testament Bible, the Koran, poetry, and readings are often included as well. Again, less is more. But it is sometimes helpful to have other's wisdom and words when you are at a loss for your own.

The Internet has many sites with appropriate quotes and inspiration. Go to your favorite search engines with key words such as "quotes on death," and "angel-on-my-shoulder." My all-time favorite source for conventional wisdom, *Bartlett's Book of Quotations* is both online and in bookstores.

Here are some quotes that I find profound, inspirational, and even humorous, for laughter leavens sorrow. Or be serious and sincere, not somber. Explain why you've chosen a particular quote, perhaps the words or the source make it the perfect epitaph for the person they knew and loved. For example, was she beyond busy and more spiritual than religious? Then, perhaps...

> Because I could not stop for death
> He kindly stopped for me
> The carriage held but just ourselves
> And immortality
>
> —Emily Dickinson

Or was he a beloved but irascible and cantankerous old codger?

I am ready to meet my Maker. Whether my
Maker is prepared for the great ordeal of meeting
me is another matter.

—Winston Churchill

Other appropriate quotes might include:
To die will be an awfully big adventure.

—Sir James Barrie, *Peter Pan*

Do not seek death. Death will find you. But seek
the road which makes death a fulfillment.

—Dag Hammarskjöld

When you were born, you cried and the world
rejoiced.
Live your life in a manner so that when you die
the world cries and you rejoice.

—Native American proverb

Seeing death as the end of life is like seeing the
horizon as the end of the ocean.

—David Searls

The gods conceal from men the happiness of
death, that they may endure life.

—Lucan

Death...the last sleep? No the final awakening.

—Walter Scott

For death begins with life's first breath
And life begins at touch of death

　　　　　　　　—John Oxenham

Here is the test to find whether your mission on
earth is finished: If you're alive, it isn't.

　　　　　　　　—Richard Bach

At a recent funeral I attended, there was a particularly
comforting quote from Helen Steiner Rice printed on the front
of the Memorial Order of Service. If you decide to speak a
poem, keep the meaning, but take words out if they tie your
tongue. Many poems are written for the eye and not the ear.

Practice for as much time as you have, until you know how
you want to deliver it, where to pause and what words need
emphasis to give the correct meaning. Slowing down and letting the words and significance sink into an audience *always*
helps.

When I must leave you
For a little while,

Please do not grieve

Or shed wild tears
And hug your sorrow to you
Through the years,

But start out bravely
With a smile.

And for my sake
And in my name,
Live on and do
All things the same.

Feed not your loneliness
On empty days,
But fill each waking hour

In useful ways.

Reach out your hand in comfort
And in cheer,

I, in turn, will comfort you
And hold you near.

And never, never
Be afraid to die,

For I am waiting for you
In the sky.

Perhaps the widow had chosen these words to help her young children and the audience, too, deal with the extra burden of an early death.

On that occasion, I quoted Henry David Thoreau: "We have lived not in proportion to the number of years we have spent, but in proportion as we have enjoyed." Also, from Ralph Waldo Emerson, "It is not length of life, but depth of life." And the Roman playwright, Lucius Seneca: "Our care should not be to have lived long as to have lived enough."

Then I related how this man had lived the years he was given to the fullest, what he cared most deeply about, and all the things that he enjoyed. With the quotes as my guide and repeating key words such as enjoy, depth, and living, the eulogy flowed simply and logically.

It is an honor to be asked to speak at such an occasion, so take care to be particularly sensitive to whatever the situation is.

For example, the friends of someone whose life had been particularly hard or challenged by drugs or alcohol might appreciate a minister's recollection of the prolific author and historian Elbert Hubbard's words: "God will not look you over for medals, degrees or diplomas, but for scars." He followed it by an explanation that it is through our wounds that we learn and heal.

And the more relevant your choice of source or words of wisdom, the better. Perhaps the poignancy of Thoreau would be appropriately paraphrased for an environmentalist or nature lover: "I went to the woods because I wished to live deliberately. To see if I could not learn what life had to teach and not, when I came to die, discover that I had not lived."

What scientist, doctor, mathematician, or even rabbi would not appreciate the sentiments of Albert Einstein at their funerals: "There are only two ways to live your life. One is as though nothing is a miracle. The other as though everything is."

And as the time comes to eulogize the Greatest Generation, all the men who lived and fought through World War II, George S. Patton, Jr.'s words add power and poignancy: "It is foolish and wrong to mourn the men who died. Rather we should thank God that such men lived."

A eulogy doesn't have to be only poems or quotes. Sometimes, songs are a Godsend, either for the lyrics or perhaps the group was a favorite of the deceased. For example, the lyrics of Three Dog Night's 1970s hit, *Never Been To Spain*: "Well I've never been to Heaven, but I've been to Oklahoma. They tell me I was born there..." could be adapted for your deceased, whether she was born in Colorado, Sarasota, or Kansas City or you were college roommates in the 70s.

A favorite hymn of mine seems particularly appropriate when there's a casket or the sprinkling of ashes from a boat or the beach.

"Oh, Lord...my boat's left on the shoreline behind me. Now with You, I'll explore other seas."

And what Irishman or boy named Daniel hasn't heard these Frederic Edward Weatherly lyrics all his life?

Oh Danny boy, the pipes, the pipes are calling
From glen to glen, and down the mountain side
The summer's gone, and all the flowers are dying
'Tis you, 'tis you must go and I must bide.

But come ye back when summer's in the meadow
Or when the valley's hushed and white with snow
'Tis I'll be here in sunshine or in shadow
Oh Danny boy, oh Danny boy, I love you so.

And if you come, when all the flowers are dying
And I am dead, as dead I well may be
You'll come and find the place where I am lying
And kneel and say an "Ave" there for me.

And I shall hear, tho' soft you tread above me
And all my dreams will warm and sweeter be
If you'll not fail to tell me that you love me
I'll simply sleep in peace until you come to me.
I'll simply sleep in peace until you come to me.

Or take something you've read in a book that seems profound. Expounding on wisdom from the current addition to the best-selling One-Minute series, *The One Minute Apology*, seemed appropriate for a wake at which I was asked to speak, with draped coffin and a burial.

I said, "No matter who wins at Monopoly, when the game is over, it all goes back in the box...the money, the property, all the Chances you took, even your game piece. All any of us get to keep is our soul, where we store whom we loved and who loved us."

Your job as a eulogizer is to add appropriate color to the play-by-play. And for Heaven's sake, if you have an appropriate and favorite poem, quote, or song that you would like shared at your own memorial, take some of the pressure off others by writing it down and sharing it with the close friends you know will be there.

One woman I know, not wanting to leave her service to chance, has scripted, choreographed, and even paid for it all in advance. Among other things, this middle-aged Yuppie wants a guitarist singing an adapted version of Peter, Paul and Mary's folk song, first released in 1966 "When I Die"...with the refrain:

And when I die and when I'm dead, dead and gone,
There'll be one child born and a world to carry on,
to carry on.

—Laura Nyro

Index

About the Author

Following the wisdom that one must stand up and live, before she can sit down to write, Anne Cooper Ready has been giving confidence in communication since 1981. Her company, Ready for Media, coaches corporate clients in making appearances in person and through the media. She has also taught the subject to UCLA's Anderson Graduate School of Business and to both national and international audiences from Los Angeles to D.C., Munich to Hong Kong.

Beginning her career as a writer for the *Chicago Tribune*, *Ad Age*, and the *Los Angeles Times*. Ms. Ready was also an associate producer for Regis Philbin before he made people millionaires.

In recent years, she has been interviewed for the Japanese-language newspaper *Yomiuri*, Paris-based *Le Figaro*, *The Times of London*, the *Montreal Gazette*, and the German-language magazine *Markt & Technik*. Ms. Ready regularly speaks to groups about issues involving corporate and crisis communications, leadership, business etiquette, international protocol, plus media as a communications tool.

Ready for Media's worldwide client list includes executives of such companies as Alcatel, Apple Computer, Clairol,

Disney, Dolby, Georgia Pacific, Hewlett Packard, Imagine Entertainment, JPL, LSI Logic, M&M Mars, Merrill Lynch, Microsoft, National Semiconductor, NOKIA, Northrop Grumman, PacifiCare, *People Magazine*, Paramount, Pepsico, Philips Electronics, Procter & Gamble, and Sempra.

Made in the USA
Lexington, KY
07 April 2010